SCARLET MARK

Cavalieri Della Morte

LEXI C. FOSS

Editing by: Outthink Editing, LLC

Alpha Reading By: Allison Irwin

Proofreading By: Barb Jack, Joy Di Biase-Giachino & Katie Schmahl

Cover Design: Jay Aheer, Simply Defined Art

Photography: CJC Photography

Models: David Wills & Riley Rebecca

Published by: Ninja Newt Publishing, LLC

Print Edition

ISBN: 978-1-950694-03-7

DEDICATION

To Dani, for giving me the opportunity to create Killian Bedivere. That means you have infinite borrowing rights. Be good to him. He likes knives.

And to Cora, for letting me play with Nikolai. You and Ava can have him back now. ;)

WARNING

Dear Reader,

Scarlet Mark is a dark romantic suspense novel with violent undertones that may contain triggers for abuse victims. Killian and Amara's relationship is unconventional—he's an assassin and she's his mark, which creates disturbing situations. This book is not recommended for those who prefer lighter romance. Killian loves his knives, in and out of the bedroom.

Enjoy xx
Lexi

PROLOGUE

Nikolai leaned one leather-clad elbow against the bar top, angled his body toward me, and cocked a dark brow. "So, you want to tell me how you convinced Calthorpe to help Ava?"

I knocked back my scotch and set the glass down. "Did I do that?"

"You tell me."

"Why don't you ask Ava?" I suggested casually, ignoring his penetrating stare. Nikolai exuded a lethal air, one that caused everyone around us to keep a wide berth. But he didn't scare me. Never had. That was what made us such good friends. From that first night in this very bar, we'd bonded over a mutual respect for the other's deadly talents.

"I did," he replied, his voice flat. "She won't tell me shit. Claims she doesn't know anyone named Dagger."

My lips twitched. "Yeah? Fancy that."

"Come on, man. Tell me what happened."

I shook my head. "Sorry, Nik. You know I don't kiss and tell."

He snorted and snatched up his glass to down the contents. "You're an ass."

"I am," I agreed, signaling the bartender for another round with a flick of my wrist. "But I'll admit, your Ava is slowly winning me over."

"I thought you didn't know each other?"

"We don't," I replied, not missing a beat. "But you've certainly told me all about her." The woman had caused him quite a bit of trouble over the years. Hence the reason I didn't like her. At least not until recently. Still… "I'm surprised you forgave her."

He sighed. "Yeah, it's quite a story, actually."

"Color me intrigued." My phone vibrated in my pocket while I spoke, forcing me to pause before I could request an explanation. "Ah, damn." The contents on the screen had me sighing and shaking my head. "Seems our reunion is being cut short." Arthur had me on a midnight flight out of Miami, giving me—I glanced at my watch—ninety minutes to get to the airport.

"Mission?" he guessed as I signaled the bartender

again.

"Yeah." A missing-person case. Pretty cut and dried, apart from the client's name. One glance at it confirmed why I'd been assigned. Mingling with the world's elite was my specialty, thanks to my family name. "Can we close our tab?" I asked as the bartender approached. Fortunately, she'd not yet poured our next round.

"Sure, babe," she replied, sounding disappointed.

I didn't bother considering why, just focused on my best friend. "This reunion isn't over. I still want the details."

"How about I give you the abridged version while I drive you to Miami International?"

Handing the bartender a few large bills that more than covered our tab, I nodded. "A solid plan." Especially as he had the car, not me. "I want to hear all about how Ava brought you to your knees."

He chuckled. "Just wait, man. You'll have your day."

"Not fucking likely." I enjoyed my single life. No one to report to other than myself. It made me the boss in every way that mattered.

"We'll see." He clapped me on the back. "Let's go."

KILLIAN

Three weeks.

Three. God. Damn. Weeks.

That was how long it took me to track down Amara fucking Rose. The woman had disappeared without a trace, something I usually would have admired if it hadn't been my task to find her.

And to end up here, of all places.

Diavolo Rojo.

My lips curled, amused by her employment choice. She'd been right under my nose this entire time. Clever female.

A string of these exclusive clubs existed across the world, designed for men and women with wealth and status who desired discretion in their sexual exploits. The *Diavolo Rojo* circuit only hired females with specific backgrounds. Most were young, early twenties, still in school, and

looking to socialize with the elite of the world. It served as a fucked-up mentorship of sorts, but it worked.

The establishment was essentially a swinger's paradise, a way to mingle and indulge in certain proclivities in a safe space with desirable partners. Although, not all of the staff played with the clients. Some tended the bar area only, enjoying the admiration of society's rich and famous while rubbing elbows with future business partners.

The women who preferred only social activities wore a special collar.

Amara Rose, my target, wasn't wearing such a collar.

Which meant I could proposition her. In any way I desired.

Such a devious woman. She'd used the funds she'd stolen from her jilted fiancé to finance this little venture—to provide herself with a new background. To qualify for employment.

That was how I finally found her.

By following the money.

"Your drink, Mr. Bedivere," a sultry voice murmured, handing me the top-shelf scotch I'd ordered. The brunette's tits practically poured out of her translucent top, leaving everything on display for my perusal.

Yet it was the auburn-haired woman tending to tables across the room who held my interest.

I'd been watching her all night, captivated by her confidence and poise. The female had conned a US senator, one many dubbed to be the future president of the United States. And she clearly did not give a flying fuck.

So damn intriguing.

And colorful. Those tattoos dancing up her left arm were the kinds of patterns meant to entice a man's tongue.

Maybe later.

I accepted my glass with a smile for the flirty waitress, saying nothing in reply. Her round eyes crinkled at the sides, her anticipation tangible as she slowly turned to present me with her delectable backside.

Cute, but not really my type.

My interests ran darker, more sinister in nature. An urge I rarely satisfied because so few met my requirements.

Although, my gorgeous mark might fit the bill.

It really was a shame that I had to kidnap her or kill her.

I sipped my scotch, enjoying the view of Amara's shapely ass as she bent to hand someone a drink in one of the corner booths.

The main area of the club resembled a standard bar, with a few opulent enhancements—crystal glassware, imported leather seating, and high-tech tabletops. The lighting offered a sexy vibe as well, casting the room in purples and shadows that set the mood.

Yet, it was the upstairs and downstairs levels that were special, each equipped with a variety of rooms and spaces set up to handle an array of kink and deviant preferences.

Amara seemed to be avoiding those, electing to serve in the safe zone, where couples chose to warm up rather than play.

I traced the device in the center of my table with my thumb, considering my mark. Several patrons had submitted bids for Amara's services throughout the evening, something I knew because each one caused the bracelet around her wrist to light up. Her staying on this floor meant she'd turned down every single one. That was part of the club's rules—the female assets controlled their fates. Hence, my brunette waitress's eagerness. She wanted me to make her an offer.

Alas, no.

My proposal would be to the alluring redhead wearing the sexy-as-fuck lace stockings and silky black teddy.

And it would be one she couldn't refuse.

I pulled out my phone to review all the other bids Amara had received tonight, thankful for my contact who had provided me with backdoor access to the club's systems. It served as potential blackmail against enemies, and in this case, access into Amara's thought process.

She had a few hard limits—something her profile indicated.

What wasn't listed was her desired price. But I had an idea of what she needed, given how much she stole from Senator Jenkins, how much she spent on this new identity of *Scarlet Rosalind*.

I flicked through the proposals she'd acquired over the last several nights. She'd declined all of them.

Difficult and confident, I mused, grinning. *My kind of woman. Let's play.*

I keyed in an amount ten times as much as her highest submission, requesting only a dance in one of the exclusive rooms downstairs. Then I checked the box for *Additional Service Negotiations Accepted*. Which meant, if things went well, we could discuss prolonging our time together and doing other, more expensive activities. In private.

My name—my *real* name—was displayed on the

sender line, the terms all laid out.

She'd be able to see my history from other *Diavolo Rojo* clubs, including the ratings her overseas colleagues had left for me. All excellent scores because they were my informants, not my conquests.

I avoided mixing business with pleasure because I was one of the villains who used those interludes to my advantage. Powerful people had a tendency to discuss private matters when in the company of beautiful women, and my contacts were brilliant at exploiting those moments. I also paid them handsomely for it. Attending the club was just a cover, an easy way to hold a covert meeting with some trusted informants.

Not that Amara would be able to review that part of the equation. She would only see I typically requested dances and rarely anything more. And I always behaved. At least on the surface.

Selecting Send, I set the device on the table and lifted my scotch.

Her wrist lit up seconds later, indicating she'd just received another request—my request.

Amara's slender shoulders tightened just enough to show her discomfort, but when she read through the offer on the wristwatch face of her bracelet, her lips actually parted.

Such a beautiful, fuckable mouth.

I could see why the senator actually desired her alive. Putting this woman in the ground would be a crime against humanity. Not that she didn't deserve it. She'd ditched the man at the altar and ran off with half of his bank account. A con woman with expert skill.

Mmm, perfection, really. How I adored vindictive women.

She nibbled her plump lower lip, her gaze scanning the room. As if I would make this easy on her. Someone like Amara required the mystery to accept such a fate.

All she could see of me was a silhouette—my all-black suit blending into the dark edges surrounding me. I'd chosen this spot because it provided me with me a full view of the room and placed a solid wall to my back.

And it shadowed my face from most of the room.

The ideal vantage point for an assassin.

Me.

Indecision warred across her features, her confidence finally wavering. Fascinating. It seemed my little vixen didn't want to be alone with male customers. Did she prefer women? Was that why she left the senator so easily?

Hmm, no, because she'd also received several offers from couples looking to add a third.

She clearly had trust issues. Something I could hardly fault her for, given her chosen profession as a scam artist.

I swirled the contents in my glass, waiting.

Watching.

Grinning.

She lowered her arm, neither accepting nor declining, and proceeded to assist another table. And then another. Every few steps, pausing to glance at her wrist as if it held all the answers.

Come on, princess. Dance for me. I wanted her alone. Not necessarily a requirement, as I'd have her in my hands soon enough, but I loved a good game of cat and mouse. And this little mouse tickled my fancy.

Almost thirty minutes passed before she touched her bracelet again.

That only served to intrigue me even more. She'd nearly given up an annual salary, out of fear? Or something more?

For someone so driven by money, I'd expected this to be an easy acceptance. But her hesitation was palpable even from across the room.

I caught the exact moment she caved. It was written in the determined set of her jaw, yet undermined by the inward curve of her shoulders.

My device hummed, her acceptance flashing across the screen. *Room 47.* The space would be mine for as long as I desired it.

Instant regret colored her face as she pressed the back of her hands to her cheeks. She blew out a breath, then lowered her head with a subtle shake that piqued my interest all the more.

This would be fun.

I closed out my bill, leaving the waitress a generous tip for her valiant efforts of seduction, and slid out of the booth. Fastening the button on my jacket, I started toward the private section underground.

While every club maintained a similar layout, each location had its quirks. This was my first visit to the Amsterdam location, which boasted a much narrower design compared to the New York City and San Francisco sites.

This venue also appeared to have a much more intense dungeon scene, creating a masterful playground for voyeurs and exhibitionists. I meandered along the outskirts, careful not to disturb those around me, and found the section I desired.

Quiet hallways, soundproof rooms, minimal surveillance.

Excellent.

I pressed my thumb to the screen outside room 47 and waited for the system to register my identity. The door slid open, revealing an interior painted in a deep red with black adornments. More leather seating, a private bar stocked with crystal glasses and top-shelf liquors, warm lighting, a stereo playing soft tones, and a small coat closet. No coffee table, only a corner side table for drinks.

Perfect arrangements for a dance and other, more intimate activities.

Slipping the jacket from my shoulders, I hung it just inside the door and removed my cuff links to roll my black dress shirt to the elbows. I wanted to feel Amara's hands on me, to test her nerves. Would her palms be clammy, or would her touch be sure? Would she try to steal from me as she did from her ex-fiancé?

So many potential scenarios, each one equally enticing.

I studied the room, specifically the areas near the couch, noting each panic button situated throughout. Every club came equipped with them, all meant to alert security of a customer taking the game a little too far. Pressing one would trigger the camera in the corner to flicker on and capture the scene, for potential legal ramifications.

Unfortunately for Amara, I had a mechanism in my pocket that short-circuited the radio frequency tied to the club's alarms. She could press those buttons all night long with me in this room, and no one would come for her.

Poor darling.

How would she react? Would she scream? Would she fight?

Goose bumps danced over my arms in anticipation.

She'd played below her league for far too long. I was here to provide her with a real match, to show her how true predators dominated this game.

A light rap against the door signaled her arrival.

I leaned against the bar, waiting as she disengaged the lock outside, feigning a bored expression as the entryway slid open to reveal the scantily clad female beyond.

That teddy looked even better close-up, the black silk an alluring contrast against her pale skin and the tattoos decorating her left arm.

She stepped inside, her stiletto heels clicking over the

marble floor. And sealed her fate by allowing the door to close behind her.

I smiled. *You're mine now, princess.*

Amara Rose was worth more alive than dead.

A gentleman would allow her to choose her fate.

But I wasn't a gentleman. Just an assassin, hired to find a mark.

And I'd just acquired my target.

KILLIAN

"Mr. Bedivere." The sultry voice sent a tingle down my spine, as did the pair of gorgeous blue-green eyes that boldly met mine. "Are you enjoying your visit to Amsterdam?"

"Who says I'm visiting?" I countered, cocking my head to the side. "What's an American girl like you doing in this branch of the *Diavolo Rojo?* I expected an accent, something different from my usual fare." A complete lie. I knew all about Amara Rose, where she was from, why she'd run here. But I wanted to goad her, see how much of the truth she'd give me.

"Are you disappointed?" she asked instead, surprising me by arching an auburn brow. "I can find you a local, if that's what you're in the mood to play with."

My lips actually twitched, amused by her clever play. "No, darling. You'll do just fine. I'm just curious, is all."

She nodded. "I see. So you're a conversation man.

Preferring to talk more than getting down to business." It was a taunt, one I volleyed back in her direction with expert ease.

"Perhaps I consider this part foreplay," I murmured, pushing off the bar and approaching her slowly, my steps measured over the ground. "Maybe I enjoy easing my prey into a false sense of comfort before I bite."

She didn't move, even as I drew into her personal space, her head tilting back to maintain her hold on my gaze. "Hmm. I'm not easy prey."

"Good," I replied, closing the gap between us, showcasing my height and size over her petite frame. She didn't flinch, proving her point. Definitely not a meek damsel, no. But a confident woman with a cruel streak.

My kind of mark.

My kind of *toy*.

"What type of music do you want to dance to?" I asked her softly, curious to see how far I could push her. "Fast or slow?"

"Depends on your mood. Sir."

Feisty. I liked that. "Both have their purpose." I skimmed my knuckles up her colorful arm, adoring the smattering of goose bumps that sprouted in the wake of my touch. She put on a good act, but her body couldn't lie. Her sharp inhale was music to my ears, her dilating pupils reminiscent of a dark desire that rivaled my own. And that scrap of silk covering her gorgeous breasts showcased a set of aroused nipples that I wanted to nibble and bite while she moaned my name.

"Slow," I decided on an exhale, wanting to prolong the tension. To play. The senator wanted her alive but didn't specify in what condition. He just wanted her breathing.

I could do that. And have a little fun, too.

"Okay." The husky quality of her voice pleased me, as did the subtle tremble in her stance as she took a step toward the stereo, her shoulder brushing mine.

"Do you want a drink?" I asked, putting on an elegant exterior that belied my murderous motives.

"A water," she replied, her focus falling to the stereo.

I grinned at her choice. "Still or sparkling?"

"Still." She switched the music over to a sensual tone that had anticipation spiking through my blood. The things I planned to do to her made this so wrong, and as a result, so incredibly right.

Female marks weren't rare. Gender played no part in the crimes of others. Marks that intrigued me were what I found rare. That this one happened to be a woman, and my type, only added to the allure.

I had earned a little amusement after tracking her down.

She'd be the one paying that price.

I filled her glass before pouring another scotch for myself, then settled onto the black leather couch.

"Your notes said you prefer the clothes to remain on," she said, striding toward me.

I spread my legs for her to step between them and held out her water. She took it with one delicate hand, lifting the rim to her lips while I watched. "Unless other items are negotiated, yes." I allowed my gaze to roam over her supple form. Curvy in all the right places. Long, shapely legs designed for this very purpose. "You're the kind of woman I'd negotiate with."

"Am I?" She straddled my hips without asking, her arms circling my neck as one would a familiar lover's, her glass cool against my skin. "So what brings you to Amsterdam?"

My eyebrow lifted. "Now you want to talk?"

"I thought you considered it foreplay."

Oh, I *liked* her.

All right, darling minx. Let's see how well you do…

"I'm here on business. You?" I phrased that last word as a question when, really, it was part of my answer. *She* was my business.

Amara smiled. "It's not a very exciting story. I just finished my undergraduate degree and wanted to take a year off before attending law school. This opportunity came up and here I am."

"Here you are," I agreed, amused by her cover story. She'd gone to great lengths to craft *Scarlet Rosalind's* background, even having a diploma created with the famous Yale imprint. I'd found records of it all and was arguably impressed by the lengths she went to, to solidify this new con. Particularly because she'd been working on it for the last six months, right beneath the senator's nose.

I sipped my scotch while holding her bold gaze, my other hand hanging limply against the seat cushion beside her knee.

"What type of work do you do, Mr. Bedivere?" she asked, performing her part remarkably well. Because I knew she didn't really care. But her interest was expected, if not required, to maintain her disguise.

"Does my record in the system not answer that

question?"

"It says you're the heir to a family fortune, that you occasionally visit the New York City and San Francisco locations, and your record is clean. But it's otherwise vague, and you said you're here on business."

"Indeed I did." I took another swallow of the liquor, enjoying the way it burned my throat on the way down. Then I set it off to the side, leaving my hands free. "Perhaps I'm here on family business."

She added her glass to the table beside mine and placed her palms on my shoulders. "Somehow I doubt that." She gazed at me through thick, gorgeous lashes, her irises lacking the fear that my victims typically held for me. Of course, she didn't know a damn thing about me. Not really.

The only reason I provided my true identity for *Diavolo Rojo* was because it suited the masquerade of my everyday life. No one outside of my small circle of friends knew of my true profession. Not even my family knew. Well, apart from my brother. He knew. He just chose not to admit it.

"What do you think I do?" I asked, lightly drawing my finger along the top of her lace stockings. "What career would you give me?"

"How did your family amass their wealth?" she countered. Expertly replying to a question with a question. Definitely a professional con artist. Unfortunately for her, she was playing with the master of deception.

And I knew exactly how to trap her.

"Buying run-down corporations and organizations, repurposing them, and reselling them to the highest bidder." I shrugged. "It's not all that fascinating, but that's where my family amassed their wealth. A few property holdings, too, that provided decent return."

"Do you work for them now?"

I laughed. "No. My older brother is the one being groomed to take over Bedivere Corp." I led an entirely different life, one she would become intimately familiar with very, very soon. "And you, Scarlet? What are your hopes and dreams for the future?"

Goose bumps pebbled beneath the pads of my fingers as I drew them up and down her soft skin, from her hip to the top of her stockings, and back up again.

So delicate.

So fragile.

So easy to carve a blade into.

"I'm living in the now," she murmured, her pupils

dilating. "The right now."

"You and me both." I studied the plump curves of her mouth, the way her tongue darted out to lick them in a show of desire laced with nervousness. For all her bravado, she seemed to be unsure of how to proceed now. "Are you going to dance for me now, sweetheart?" I asked softly, slowly lifting my gaze back to hers. "Or are you desiring a negotiation?"

How far would she go? What would she ask of me? What would I allow us to do before I broke the news to her?

So many questions.

I adored them all, luxuriating in the stillness of the moment—that tender few minutes before attacking one's prey. She was right where I wanted her, falling beautifully into my trap without any realization of how numbered her seconds truly were. It made me a very bad man. And I would never apologize for it.

"You're..." She swallowed, her nails digging into the fabric clothing my shoulders. "This is my first time accepting an offer."

I almost startled at her giving me the truth, then realized her intended purpose—to twist the game. To feign an innocence a dominant male like me craved.

Such a clever, beautiful woman.

Picking up on all my cues apart from the one that mattered the most—my true intentions.

"We'll ease into it," I offered, grasping her hips with both hands. "Dance for me first. I want to see how well you move." *If you dare.*

Her lips curled enticingly. "I thought you'd never ask."

She slid from my lap, deftly balancing on her heels. I picked up my scotch again, watching her over the rim as she found the soft, rhythmic beat. She swayed, slow at first, testing the cadence of the song. It seemed rather general, if a bit boring, until she closed her eyes.

A haze of seduction fell over her, Amara's body moving to a sensual tempo that came off as natural and oozed sex. It started in her hips and lifted through her core, to her arms, to the way her head tilted back as she fell into the music.

I forgot how to swallow, entranced by her open charisma and the vulnerability spilling from her features. It wasn't her movements so much as her expression. Heartbreak and desire mingled to create the most alluring picture I'd ever seen.

Then those lashes lifted to reveal the truth inside her. Agony darkened her irises while desire cut through the dilated pinpoints of her eyes, piercing me deep. That kind of emotion could not be feigned. Nor could the faint hint of her arousal scenting the air as she spun to lower herself to my thighs and up again—brief touches, all meant to seduce, providing a sensual glimpse into what could happen between us if we gave in to the erotic pull.

I'd expected this attraction, anticipated it, but to have it dancing before me with tangible strokes had my cock hardening to a near-painful degree. This woman was temptation personified. From her clever ways to her sexy-as-fuck form, I was almost lost to her.

But I had a job to do, one that required my focus.

And if she kept dancing like that, my control might snap. Just for a second.

I returned my glass to the table, catching her gaze and giving her a tilt of my chin.

She followed the nonverbal request with a smile, straddling my hips again while still shifting to the hedonistic tones. I allowed her to continue, enjoying the way her lips parted upon feeling my clear desire, and groaned as she purposely brushed against me to show her own pleasure at finding me hard for her.

"Vixen," I breathed, impressed beyond words.

Her throaty chuckle slid over me, her palms running up and down my chest, my arms, her heated cunt a brand against my thighs.

Fucking this mark would be dangerous.

But damn if I didn't want a taste.

Alas, I was married to my job. And I never cheated.

I wove my fingers through Amara's thick, auburn hair and pulled her closer, distracting her from the movements of my opposite hand—the hand sliding the knife out of my pocket. "There's a camera in here," I whispered against her mouth.

"It's not on," she promised. "They only use it for safety precautions."

"I know." I ran my tongue over her bottom lip. "That's why I'm mentioning it." Because it could technically be turned on at any time, just to check in and ensure employee safety. And as this was Amara's first client, management might peek in to check on her status. Not because they truly cared, but because they'd want to know her capabilities. This was a sex club at its core, not a bar.

She grasped my shoulders, her hips still moving in that

sexy way across my lap. "I'm not worried."

"Mmm, but you should be." I pressed the edge of my blade into her side, just below her ribs. Hard enough to feel, yet soft enough not to cut the silk of her teddy. "I told you the truth earlier, Amara. I'm here for business, and my business, darling, is *you*."

AMARA

I froze.

Amara.

He knew my name.

My *real* name. Had said it with a certainty I felt deep in my stomach. Until the rest of his words registered.

A tremble ricocheted down my spine, my head jerking of its own accord, only to be held captive by the hand at the back of my head—a hand I'd enjoyed on me only moments ago.

"Shh," he whispered, his lips brushing mine. "Don't worry. No one will be interrupting us, but I'd very much prefer you to remain calm on the off chance someone is peeking in. I'd hate to have to kill others. I rather like the *Diavolo Rojo.*"

I forgot how to breathe, my limbs locking in place, my fingers clamped around his shoulders.

Everything went hot and cold.

My heart threatened to beat out of my chest.

Oh God. Oh God. Oh God.

What now?

Pull yourself together.

How?

You'll get out of this. You always do. You're a survivor.

But something about this man said very few survived him.

As if sensing my thoughts, he grinned. "Scared, Amara?" He nuzzled my cheek, causing me to flinch into the blade at my side. "You should be. You pissed off a very important person." He pulled back slightly, tilting his head to the side. "Do you feel bad about it?"

His words ran hot through my thoughts, searing my insides.

He works for Malcom.

He found me.

I need to run.

I can't—

"Silence?" The man beneath me tsked, his gaze holding a touch of disappointment. "And here I thought you were enjoying my brand of foreplay." The sharp edge along my side sliced through the silk of my teddy, meeting my skin and sending a shiver of dread through me.

Fight!

Not yet.

I had an escape route.

I *always* did.

But it required me to be lower, near the bottom of the couch where the safety buttons were located. This was my assigned room. I'd memorized every inch of it after my club mentor had given me the keys, saying no one else would ever use it apart from me and whomever I allowed inside. Two seconds was all I needed—

"You'll never make it," he said softly, the blade digging into my skin. "One wrong move and I'll send this dagger directly into your heart. They'll never save you in time. And I'll be so disappointed, too, because you're worth a lot more to me alive. But I'll get paid either way."

I swallowed, my heart beating a chaotic rhythm. I had not come this far only to be caught by this... this... "Who are you?" I asked, my raspy voice a harsh sound that I barely recognized. "You don't work for Malcom." I didn't recognize him as one of my former fiancé's henchmen.

"No, I don't." His dark brown irises—nearly black in

the low lighting—glimmered with sinister intent. I'd been fooled by his profile and expensive suit, the elegant way he held himself. But a lethal essence lurked beneath his black clothing, his eyes holding the windows to his evil soul.

Why were these men always the ones I found most attractive?

A consequence of my upbringing—I didn't know any better. My parents groomed me for this life, forced me into the arrangement with Malcom, and left me there to face a fate worse than death.

And now I sat astride a different sort of predator, one who told me with a glance that he was accustomed to hurting others. His threat was underlined in experience. If I moved in a way he didn't like, he'd kill me. Of that I had no doubt.

How did I miss that when I entered the room? I read people for a living; it was the skill Malcom most adored about me—if *adored* was even the right term. Maybe *found most useful* was a better description.

Regardless, I'd somehow missed this man's deadly intent. All I'd seen was interest in his features, an interest I had wholeheartedly returned. Most of the clients in this club were all-right-looking, older, and into kinky shit that surpassed my comfort zone.

Mr. Bedivere had been a welcome surprise. I recognized the name immediately, aware of his family legacy. But the elusive billionaire heir rarely allowed himself to be photographed in public.

And now I wondered if this man even was a Bedivere or if he'd stolen the identity in an elaborate ruse to catch me.

"Who are you?" I tried again, my voice slightly steadier despite my racing pulse.

His lips curled, a pair of dimples flashing that had no reason to exist on his chiseled features. It made him appear boyish. Innocent. But one more glance in his dark, open gaze proved that to be a venomous lie.

I should have paid more attention.

But my instincts didn't riot around him, not like they did around the others...

"Killian Bedivere," he said. "You'll find I've yet to lie to you."

So he was the heir to a massive fortune? "Are you friends with Malcom?" I'd never seen Killian at one of the parties. I would recognize him in a heartbeat.

"Hardly. He's just a client who requested my special

set of skills. And he's paying quite handsomely for them, too."

"Skills," I repeated, trying to lull him back into talking, since he seemed to enjoy that. Distractions were something I had mastered long ago. Escaping was another talent of mine. I just had to find the right moment. And somehow encourage him to remove the knife digging into my rib cage.

"Finding people. Killing them." He watched me carefully, as if searching for some sort of shock value. It wouldn't exist.

This man knew nothing about the horrors of my upbringing.

Yes, he'd caught me off guard.

Yes, having a blade pressed into my skin scared me.

But *he*—the man—did not.

I knew my fair share of monsters. He could join the club.

His lips curled. "It's such a shame I have to hand you over to your former betrothed. I sense you and I would have quite a bit of fun together."

The mention of Malcom made my stomach churn. "You have no idea who you're dealing with."

Killian's eyebrows—dark and gorgeously shaped— lifted. "On the contrary, princess. You have no idea who *you* are dealing with."

"You misunderstand," I said, my nails digging into his shoulders. "I mean Malcom. He's... he's not who he pretends to be."

He chuckled. "Is anyone? *Scarlet Rosalind.*"

I sighed. There was no use. No one would listen to me. No one would care. I learned a long time ago that the only person I could rely on was myself. This was no different.

"You realize it took me three weeks to track you down?" he continued. "That's a record for me."

"You're welcome," I deadpanned, eliciting a laugh from him. Glad he was so easily amused.

"Oh, I like you, Amara," he murmured, angling his head toward mine. "I know he wasn't your first con. You pulled it off too beautifully for him to be a first. So who was it? Or have you fucked up so many lives that you've lost count?"

I frowned. He thought I was a con woman? That I'd willingly entered Malcom's life to, what, steal money from him? A laugh caught in my throat. As if our past had been that easy. Maybe I wouldn't be here now, desperate enough to work in a club like *Diavolo Rojo* to earn a few bucks in exchange for my soul.

"Come now," Killian coaxed. "Entertain me at least a little bit."

"I already danced for you. That's all we negotiated." A snappy retort but I couldn't help it. This man was serving as judge, jury, and executioner—literally—without knowing a damn thing about me. "Malcom's playing you, and you don't even know it."

His eyebrows rose, then his chest shook with hilarity. "No one plays me, darling."

"There's a first time for everything," I said sweetly, my lips curling. "So how do you plan to get me out of here?" Because someone would notice me leaving against my will. This club catered to sex, but they also seemed to care about their employees. And Bridget, my mentor, was on the floor tonight. One glance her way and she'd send security after us.

"I have a present for you in my pocket," he murmured, his grip on my hair tightening. "Be a good girl and find it for me. Slowly."

The belittling endearment had my eyes narrowing. I was neither *good* nor a *girl*. But I'd happily inspect him to see what other weapons he had hidden on his person.

As if sensing my thought, his lips twitched.

I ignored his palpable amusement and slid my palms slowly over his solid chest—his muscles more than evident even through the shirt—and lower to the flat planes of his abdomen.

If he didn't have a knife to my side, I'd be far more impressed.

Because damn.

He obviously took care of himself. That, paired with his face, and, well, *lethal attraction* seemed an appropriate description. The man oozed power and sex, his gaze sinful, his smile alluring, his body… perfection.

My tongue felt too big for my mouth by the time I reached his belt. Danger and menace lurked beneath his skin, and a bad, *bad* part of me desired a taste.

Which gave me an idea.

A lesson I learned long ago was to base every plan on a truth. Lies had a way of biting a person in the ass. But a twisted idea based on realism usually provided a win in the end.

And I needed to win this game between us. My life depended on it.

"In your pocket?" I repeated, drawing my finger downward over the impressive bulge beneath his zipper. "Is that an invitation?"

His smoldering gaze held mine. "Are you trying to play, darling? Because I should warn you, I'm not easily manipulated."

I didn't doubt that for a second.

However, men were easy creatures who adored sex. And I excelled at seduction. A requirement of my upbringing.

"What time are you delivering me to Malcom?" I asked, applying subtle pressure to his groin. Just enough to tease and to show I knew how to handle him.

"Whenever I want," he replied, his voice deepening. "Dead or alive."

"But I'm worth more to you alive." The words were more for my benefit than for his. It meant he would be hesitant to stab me—at least fatally. Of course, I'd prefer to avoid it altogether.

He smiled. "You were listening. Good girl."

I'm going to enjoy hurting you, I decided, my mouth curling with the thought. "And what am I supposed to be finding?" I asked, tracing his sizable erection. Hmm, it seemed every part of him was well proportioned and enticing. Too bad he chose the wrong side of this battle. Because I agreed with him—we'd have fun with each other.

"All right, sweetheart. You want to play this game?"

I gave him my best innocent look. "Who says I'm playing?"

"Cute." He smiled, dipping his chin. "Seduce away, darling. But I won't be letting you go. I'm married to my job first and foremost. And I never fail a mission."

I believed him. He struck me as honest in an odd way, as if he relied on that as his one redeeming trait. Every bounty hunter—or whatever he called himself—needed one. At least in my experience.

"Maybe I'll be your first failure," I taunted, toying with his belt and deftly loosening the buckle.

His irises simmered, reminding me of hot chocolate. His good looks made this a little easier because I didn't have to feign my interest. Evil intentions didn't bother me. At least, not in the way they did others. So I could look past his designs for me, to the handsome male beneath the task. It was a knack I'd perfected over the years, one that would serve me well now.

I slowly leaned in to press a kiss to his throat. "This room is mine all night. If you don't have a timeline…" I let the sentence dangle between us, my tongue tracing his too-steady pulse. If this distraction was going to work, I needed his undivided attention. I needed him to become putty in my hands.

His grip tightened in my hair as he yanked me upward, his dark eyes capturing mine as I popped the button of his suit pants. The expensive wool slid against my fingers, enticing me to explore the hard length beneath.

"I know what you're doing, Amara. But if you really want to attempt to change my mind, then feel free to try." He released my hair. "I recommend using that pretty mouth, sweetheart. Make it worth my while."

Oh, I was going to enjoy this far too much.

My lips teasingly danced over his, his scotch-and-peppermint breath mingling with mine. He grinned, the sensation a taunt against my mouth. Killian didn't think I'd follow through. He was both right and wrong.

I closed the gap between us, kissing him and unleashing the gifts of my existence. Years of training. Seduction. Skill. I allowed him a taste with the tip of my tongue, slowly gliding it along his, demonstrating my power. He shivered, but the knife remained resolutely against my side while his opposite hand skimmed my spine upward to wrap around the back of my neck.

Such a dominant hold, one he punctuated by taking control of our embrace, his tongue setting the pace for mine as he returned my kiss with expert skill.

I wasn't expecting *that*.

Most men in my history seemed to have missed Kissing 101.

But not Killian.

No, he knew what he was doing and proceeded to prove it by staking his claim inside my mouth. A moan slid from my chest of its own accord, causing his grip to tighten.

I moved closer, placing my heated center over his arousal. It served as a way to take back my role, to own him, yet somehow I ended up being the one wanting more, to press myself into him.

God, this was fucked up.

He had a knife to my side, and I *wanted* him. Hell, part of me even liked it.

Focus, Amara, I told myself. *He's fucking with you.*

I ran my nails up and down his torso, delighting in the hard planes beneath his black dress shirt. His buttons loosened easily, my fingers trained in the art of removing clothing. He hissed in a breath as I touched his bare skin, my palms running over his pectorals and abdominal muscles with ease.

Why do you have to be my enemy? I wondered, almost sad. Because exploring his body with my tongue would be an enjoyment, an escape from my otherwise cruel life.

Alas, this was a required task, one I needed to accomplish to survive.

I broke our kiss, drifting my lips over his defined cheekbones to his ear, his dark strands soft against my nose. "Have I changed your mind yet?" I asked, nipping his earlobe.

"Not even close," he replied, his voice husky with want. "When I told you to use your mouth, I meant around my cock."

I smiled. "I know." I licked down to his pulse, testing the rhythm again. Slightly elevated, but mostly steady. *Not my typical target.* He posed a challenge that excited my instincts and had my legs clenching around his hips.

His cock felt like heaven between my thighs, so hot and heavy, and oh, the scrap of lace did nothing to contain my responding arousal.

I want him.

And wasn't that insane? To desire a man in these conditions, a man who wanted to give me back to a monster. But I learned to accept my less-than-conventional proclivities years ago. It was what allowed me to be, well, me.

I drew a slow path along his collarbone, licking and tasting and nibbling his smooth, tan skin. Mmm, he was delicious. Hard. Warm. Male.

"Are you going to your knees, Amara?" His voice held a rough quality that skated across my skin, scattering goose bumps down my arms. Definitely a man used to being in charge in every way. My kryptonite.

My gaze lifted to his as I licked a trail downward between his impressive pecs, my thighs sliding slowly across his legs. The blade moved with me, gliding upward along my ribs, his pupils engulfing his irises.

His grip on my neck tightened, halting my movements as I reached the base of his sternum. And the knife lifted to my throat, the razor edge a clear threat against my sensitive skin.

"Don't test me, darling. You might be worth more alive, but I will hurt you if you hurt me."

"Worried I might bite?" I teased, smiling. "Or worried

I won't?"

Intrigue darkened his features. "Oh, you're definitely playing a dangerous game."

"What's life without a little excitement?" I countered, licking my lips. "And you're the one who told me to use my mouth."

"Indeed I did." He released my neck, but the blade remained. "Continue if you dare."

Oh, I dare.

And you'll regret ever challenging me.

I almost felt bad. Not that I should. He took a job for Malcom Jenkins. Anyone who worked for that man deserved their fate.

Including what I had planned.

"I dare," I murmured, continuing my path along his perfectly sculpted abdomen.

Another day, another time, I'd have enjoyed this so much more.

But not tonight.

He held my gaze the whole way down, his nostrils flaring, the knife a steady presence against my throat. I knew he would use it. I just had to be faster.

This was my room.

I had prepped it knowing I may need to escape.

And poor, gorgeous Killian was about to learn a valuable lesson.

Never fuck with a woman who has nothing to lose.

A woman like me.

My knees hit the ground, and he spread his legs to allow me to settle between them. The dagger slid to the side of my neck, his hand appearing as a caress to the camera should someone peek in on us. A clever man. Trained. Obviously used to having to cover his tracks.

I pressed a kiss to his lower abdomen, above the black boxer briefs that no doubt fit him gloriously well. My palms skimmed his toned thighs, adoring the strength beneath the soft fabric, and settled near his loosened belt and unsnapped button. Catching the zipper in my teeth, I guided it downward, our gazes locked on one another the whole time.

Curiosity mated with lust as he watched me, his expression heated, his free hand falling to his ripped stomach. I grabbed his pants and gave them a tug, pulling them down, while smiling up at him.

This was the moment I desired.

The play I'd been waiting for. And his gaze said he

knew it, anticipated it, was curious to see what I would do.

But he had no way of knowing.

Guiding the fabric over his knees, my knuckles brushed the edge of the couch. His lips twitched, the blade against my throat admirably steady. But he'd rested it against the side, not the base. Just as I desired. I shifted higher on my knees, my hands closer to his calves now, and pretended to adjust to finish removing his pants.

If I really wanted him distracted, I could continue the job.

But something told me he'd never let his guard down, no matter how fantastic my mouth might feel around him.

Now or never.

I slid my palm beneath the couch, finding the item I required, securing it, and smiling up at him as he lifted a knowing brow.

"The panic buttons won't work, sweetheart," he murmured, clearly having felt my touch leave his leg. "But nice try."

I feigned disappointment. "What do you mean they 'won't work'?"

"Check my pants pocket, like I asked before."

Frowning, I glanced down. His gaze followed, which

was precisely what I wanted. A simple distraction that provided me with the means to react.

I shifted to the side—away from his blade—and lifted my hand at the same time. I only had one chance to make this work.

I didn't even think. I just acted. Slamming my fist into his exposed thigh, I dug the needle deep into his skin and pressed down on the contents with my thumb before leaping backward. His knife had caught me on the chin, my movements too unexpected and fast for him to keep up with to make the cut deadly.

"Cute," he said, eyeing the item in his thigh. "Very fucking cute."

"You won't be saying that in about a minute," I told him, taking another step back as he pulled the needle out and tossed it aside.

He stood and pulled up his pants, fastening them with a speed that actually impressed me.

"What is it?" he asked, all signs of playfulness gone. "What did you just inject into me?"

I swallowed. "You'll see soon enough." It wouldn't kill him. Just give him a nice little nap.

He advanced on me so fast I couldn't get out of his

way in time. But it wasn't his blade he put at my throat, just his hand. "That was a bad move, little girl." He slid his hand into his pocket, then blinked and shook his head. "*Fuck.*"

It's working. For a moment I thought maybe I'd done it wrong, that maybe—

His hand tightened around me, his knife appearing again.

And I reacted.

I couldn't help it.

My knee went upward right between his thighs, landing in the sweet spot and eliciting a harsh curse from his lips. His grip loosened just enough for me to twist away from him. He took a dangerous step toward me, shaking his head again, and I danced out of his reach.

"What the fuck ish ith?" he slurred.

"A sedative," I whispered, jumping backward as he fell to his knees. He'd be fine. This was only temporary.

I need to get the fuck out of here.

He said my name as I put my hand on the doorknob. Nothing else followed.

I risked a glance back at him and found his dark gaze on me, not angry, but devastatingly amused. He *liked* that

I'd bested him. I couldn't help my smile.

"Was that as good for you as it was for me?" I asked.

His lips twitched and he collapsed, immobilized.

"Bye, Killian."

AMARA

Money.

Bag.

IDs.

I ran through the mental checklist several times while wandering through *Amsterdam Centraal.* My train was scheduled to depart just before five o'clock in the morning, straight to Berlin. From there, I'd hop on a flight or another train and keep moving until I figured out what to do and where to go.

Fucking Killian Bedivere. How did he find me? I'd paid an exorbitant sum for Scarlet Rosalind's identity. It'd been airtight.

Collapsing into my seat on the train, I pinched the bridge of my nose between my fingers and tossed my bag onto the floor. I'd not brought much, just two outfits, cash, and some identification.

My tank top clung to my skin beneath my brown jacket, my jeans pasted onto my legs. And my boots had seen better days.

But I couldn't afford to bring anything else with me. This was my existence now.

And fuck, I was exhausted.

Sad.

Relieved.

This life was not what I had intended. But I couldn't go back to Malcom. I'd rather die first. The things he wanted me to do, the things he *forced* me to do, were worse than any death Killian could bestow upon me.

And the things Malcom wanted to do…

I quivered, not wanting to revisit those memories. The famous senator was a vile man behind closed doors. But only a few saw that side of him.

Unluckily for me, I was among those few.

Suppressing a shudder, I tried to relax in my seat, waiting for the train to start rolling. The sooner the better. I'd drugged Killian a few hours ago, so he would definitely be awake now, and lucid.

And probably pissed.

Malcom will punish him for failing.

A shiver of unease pulsed through my being. I never meant to bring anyone else into this mess. Not that I'd invited Killian into my life. That lay at Malcom's feet. Technically, everything did. That man was a heinous piece of—

"Berlin?" a deep voice drawled as a now-familiar man took the seat beside me, blocking my one and only exit into the aisle. The window to my right didn't open, not that I could jump through it anyway. Because the train had just started moving.

Oh, fuck...

"That's almost, what, six and a half hours?" he continued, his lips curling. "Plenty of time for us to catch up, yeah?"

"H-how?" I breathed. I'd knocked him out cold. Left him at *Diavolo Rojo*. Didn't return to my home, but instead went to the locker that held my escape kit. Killian Bedivere should not have been able to follow me. I'd mapped this out perfectly, had my ticket purchased in cash on-site. No tracking. No visibility. My hair was in a ponytail beneath a hat, my clothes street-appropriate and meant to blend in with a crowd. He should not have been able to find me.

"Oh, Amara," he sighed. "This is what I do for a living.

I always have contingency plans in place." He grabbed my forearm, sliding a bracelet around my wrist and closing it before I could even think to react. "There. That's better. Now you're mine."

I flinched my arm away from him, the skin burning from where he'd touched me. And glowered at the metal cuff. "What the fuck?"

"You know, I love technology." He opened his palm to reveal a remote of some kind. "Run off and I'll press this button. Trust me, you don't want that to happen."

My blood chilled. "What?"

"It's similar to a tagging device, only more lethal." He shrugged, sliding the gadget into his jacket pocket. He'd changed out of the suit, donning black jeans, a blood-red sweater, and a leather coat. "Now, where were we? Oh, right, you knocked me out with a drug. I really hope that needle was clean, Amara, or you're going to regret ever meeting me."

"I already regret it."

His lips curled into a handsome grin. "Don't tease me, darling. I'm still rather hot and bothered from our playtime last night." He winked at me and bent to pick up my bag from the floor. I reached for it, but he tsked. "Naughty,

Amara. What will I do with you?"

Killian's words struck me in the gut, sending me back to a night in Malcom's basement. To his displeasure at my lackluster performance.

My cheek stung from the imprint of his palm, my sides aching from the exertion of remaining in a kneeling position. I'd done what he asked, what he demanded of me. But not to his satisfaction.

"What part of 'find out what he knows' don't you get?" he demanded. "You're supposed to suck his cock, or do whatever other activity he asks. Then prod him while he's in a state of bliss. Your guardians promised me you were well trained in the art of sexual interrogation, but I'm really starting to think you're broken." He took a long drag on his cigar, sighing. "Perhaps it's a performance issue."

"I tried and he—"

Malcom grabbed a handful of my hair, yanking my head backward to meet his cold gaze. "Did I say I wanted an explanation?"

"N-no, sir," I managed on a stutter, my throat burning from a lack of water. He'd kept me chained down here for too long, furious that I hadn't been able to obtain the details he needed from Representative Bryce. All the man wanted

to do was fuck my mouth, which made asking questions difficult. And he wasn't the type to cuddle afterward.

"Oh, Amara. What will I do with you?" Malcom asked on a sigh, his blue eyes glimmering with ideas. All of them malicious. All of them designed to hurt. "I have a client meeting tomorrow. Perhaps I'll lay you out naked across the table, let them—"

"Passports and tickets," a gruff voice announced, shaking me from the dark memory. I could still feel the hands on me from that subsequent meeting, still taste them all on my tongue.

"Killian with Europol," my companion said in fluent German, handing the man a black wallet. "I'm escorting this woman back to Berlin for trial."

My lips parted. *What?*

"Oh?" The border agent flipped the top to review the badge inside.

Seriously?

Killian pulled a folded sheet of paper from his jacket pocket, holding it out for the officer. "Do you need her passport? It's in this bag somewhere." He jostled the backpack—*my* backpack—on his lap. He hadn't gone through it yet, so his statement was a guess. An accurate one, but still a leap of faith.

"That won't be needed, Officer Killian," the slender male replied. "Do you need help with detainment?"

Killian chuckled. "Nah, she's harmless. Doesn't even need cuffs."

The border patrol agent nodded and handed back his wallet. "Let me know if that changes."

"Of course," he replied smoothly, tucking the still-folded paper back into his pocket, followed by his badge. "Have a nice day."

The man gave another nod and moved on to the next set of passengers several rows away.

"Officer Killian?" I repeated, arching an eyebrow. "And what trial am I attending in Berlin?"

"You speak German?" he countered.

I snorted. "That's your question?" I didn't speak it well, but I understood it. In addition to several other languages. "So you work for Europol?" I asked.

He smirked. "Today I do." He dropped my bag onto the floor and turned toward me, his gaze boring into mine. "What was in the syringe?"

I chewed my cheek, debating if I wanted to answer that. Mostly because I didn't owe him a damn thing. But it wasn't like I'd spiked him full of an illegal drug.

"Ketamine. What they use to sedate horses and unruly patients, or in your case, headstrong men." The last part was added in a saccharine tone meant to irritate him.

"I know what ketamine is, sweetheart." His gaze glittered. "But I'll admit to that being my first time on the receiving end of it. Talk about a hallucinogenic trip. Remind me to return the favor."

"Well, unlike you, it wouldn't be my first time," I muttered, rotating to stare out the window, the weight of the situation finally falling on my shoulders.

He found me.

Again.

And not only that, but he'd also clamped some sort of device around my wrist. Solid steel, from the feel of it, but with something lethal encased inside the metal walls. What would it do? Explode? Emit a toxin?

A biological weapon? my mind whispered, sending a chill of a memory down my spine. *He's taking me back to* him.

Malcom.

My worst nightmare.

Oh, he wouldn't kill me. No. He'd deliver me to a far

worse fate. Maybe auction me off to the highest bidder, or pass me around to his friends, without rules this time. Because his favorite little toy had disobeyed him. That made me defective. Broken. A disloyal plaything.

I swallowed. *This can't be the end.* I couldn't just give up. I had to fight. Going back to Malcom was a destiny I refused to accept.

But how? I needed a new plan, a way to remove this device from my wrist, a way to get rid of Killian.

It wouldn't be so easy this time. I'd already shown a handful of my cards, and he'd swept the deck right out from under me.

"Yes," his deep voice said beside me. "Berlin." I glanced back at him, frowning, then noticed the phone at his ear. "Six or so hours." He glanced at his watch and nodded. "Yes." Whomever he spoke to said something else that had him snorting. "Not a problem." Another nod. "Will do." He ended the call and relaxed into his chair. "I need a fucking nap. Be a sweetheart and don't move for a while."

"Where would I go?" I asked softly, returning my focus to the window.

This man had me in his custody until Berlin.

That gave me a few hours to come up with a plan,

some way to evade him. I knew Berlin, had been there countless times.

I can do this, I told myself. *I have to.*

Because the alternative was unfathomable.

I'd die before I let Malcom touch me again.

KILLIAN

Drugs weren't something I experimented much with as a kid or an adult, but fuck if that ketamine didn't take me on a wild ride. It made sleeping impossible because every time I closed my eyes, some strange phantom stared back at me.

Damn woman had knocked me fully off-kilter. Which earned her a smidgen of respect. Not only had she eluded me for weeks, but she'd also bested me.

It would not be happening again.

She remained quiet beside me, but I could practically hear her mind working. Part of me was thrilled by the thought of another escape attempt, curious to see how she'd finagle her way out of my grasp. The other part of me knew it was impossible.

That device on her wrist could only be removed by my thumbprint.

And it would not only explode at my request, but it would also track her.

Being a member of the Tabella Della Morte paid off. Literally. I had access to all the best toys, and my bank account afforded me the opportunity to play with them. Even the items that weren't available to government agencies yet, such as that beauty around her wrist.

My pocket buzzed with an incoming message about the car I'd ordered. I eyed the details with a grin. One perk of being in Germany? The Autobahn. And Senator Jenkins had requested a pickup location outside of the city for later tonight, giving me a prime excuse for a drive in the new toy.

Maybe I'd take a vacation afterward, roaming around Europe for a while. I had friends in various places. Could be a worthwhile holiday.

And boring as hell. Especially after the last few days.

Amara Rose had become my obsession, one I had enjoyed more than any other mark in my history. Handing her over to Jenkins's men would suck. But I couldn't prolong our time together after it took me so long to track her down. The senator wanted his fiancée back.

What would he do to her?

Punish her?

Kill her?

I frowned at that last bit. No. He wouldn't murder her after paying so much for her to be caught alive—a rarity in my line of work.

As if sensing my train of thought, she wrapped her arms around her middle, her shoulders hunching. Several hours of plotting seemed to have worn her out, or maybe she'd finally accepted that there was no escape.

No, she wouldn't cave that easily. This woman was a fighter. She actually reminded me a bit of myself, refusing to accept fate when it stared her right in the face.

"Why did you con one of the country's most beloved senators?" I wondered. "Was it a rite of passage of sorts? A graduation to a new level? I mean, what prompted it?"

Her eyes appeared greener in the daylight, the shades of blue receding to the areas around her pupils. "You assume I conned him."

"Didn't you?" I pressed. That was what the senator implied.

She shrugged. "Everyone lies about something."

A vague statement, one I could easily hear myself saying. "So tell me a truth," I dared. "Tell me something real."

"Why?"

"Because I spent the last three weeks tracking your whereabouts and I want to know a truth outside your world of fiction."

She laughed, but it lacked humor. "A truth." She shook her head. "Malcom might be a beloved senator on the surface, but a devil lurks beneath his skin. I wouldn't be surprised if he double-crosses you in some way, either."

"That's not something about you," I pointed out while filing away the subtle warning.

My read on the senator had raised a few red flags. However, Calthorpe assured me he was a solid client. Of course, all the leader of the Tabella Della Morte cared about was being paid. Oh, his Cavalieri—like me—were his trusted knights, but Arthur Calthorpe did not have an emotional bone in his body. It was something I admired about him, his coldhearted will to rule us all. But it also kept me on constant guard.

"Come on, princess," I urged. "Give me something to remember you by."

"The ketamine wasn't enough?" she asked coyly.

"Oh, that definitely provided a lasting memory." I

leaned into her space. "As was the sensation of your hot cunt against my leg. But I want to know something *real* about you."

She licked her bottom lip. "Having me nearly naked in your lap wasn't intimate enough for you?"

I grinned. "Well, it certainly left me craving more." Her little seductive game climaxed in her obtaining the upper hand, intriguing me all the more. "Give me something, Amara."

"I owe you nothing."

"I let you live."

"You say that as if it's a mercy, but if you knew the hell I was returning to, you'd realize that's not the case at all."

Interesting. "Then why choose him as your mark?"

"Who says I chose him?"

I scoffed. "So, what, someone else put you up to it?"

"Again, you're making assumptions about intentions you don't understand." Her gaze held mine. "I'm not a con woman, Killian. Consider that my truth."

She spoke with such confidence, such certainty. If I hadn't seen the financial proof of what she'd done to Senator Jenkins, I'd almost believe her. "You ran off with half his bank account, Amara."

She snorted. "One bank account of several. And trust me, it hardly made a dent in his net worth."

That explained how he was paying the Tabella Della Morte so handsomely for this job. I'd wondered how he could afford our rates with a diminished account.

"Regardless, you still stole money from him. After leaving him at the altar." The public embarrassment alone was enough to tarnish the good senator's reputation. Of course, his publicist spun it in his favor by proclaiming him to be brokenhearted and single again.

Which meant he didn't intend to take Amara back.

So what did he have planned for her?

I shook my head. It wasn't for me to worry about. This was a job, and she deserved her fate. End of discussion.

Amara seemed to agree, as she remained quiet, her hands curled into fists as we approached our final destination in Berlin. I could practically hear the wheels turning inside that delicious mind of hers, plotting her escape. Alas, she had no chance. Not with that device on her wrist. And I also knew this city forward and backward. She had nowhere to go, nowhere to hide.

The announcement of our arrival had Amara stiffening beside me.

"You'll follow me," I told her. "Or I'll show you what that device around your wrist can do."

"You need me alive," she reminded me, a smirk in her voice.

"That I do." I leaned into her, pressing my lips to her ear. "I didn't say the device would kill you, did I?" I suppose I had used the term *lethal*, which was true. But it had varying degrees of electrical therapy tied to it.

A shock wrist cuff designed for humans.

Brilliant.

She didn't seem nearly as amused, her gaze falling. Poor thing. I almost pitied her.

"Shouldn't have fucked with the senator, darling," I murmured, using my thumb to tug her bottom lip from between her teeth. "The price of betrayal can be steep."

"You have no idea," she whispered, shaking her head and knocking my hand away in the process. "No fucking idea."

"Ah, but I do." I'd seen a lot in my twenty-eight years. Typically, I was hired to deliver justice, but this wasn't my first time retrieving a mark for the client's brand of punishment.

However, this was my first time feeling a niggling of

regret for having to hand over a target to the customer.

Only because I enjoyed this task so much.

I'd have to ask Arthur for another.

"Let's go," I said as the train stopped. Her bag went over my shoulder as I stood, my hand held out for hers. She begrudgingly gave me her palm, her skin clammy against my own. A nervous tell that informed me she had a plan up her sleeve.

Bring it on, darling.

I linked my fingers through hers, dragging her along at my side off the train and into the crowds of Berlin Central Station. The car I ordered was in the Hauptbahnhof parking garage. I just had to pick up the keys from my delivery man.

Amara remained quiet but vigilant, her steps measured and sure.

I searched the crowd for the sign I desired and smiled when I spotted the one that read "Mister Dagger."

Greeting the male in fluent German, I flashed my identification and thanked him as he handed me the keys to a brand-new Audi R8. Sleek, gorgeous, perfection with enough horsepower to send us flying toward our destination. I couldn't wait to feel her purr beneath me.

The same could be said about my charge, who had yet to say a word.

"You're being awfully well behaved," I commented, squeezing her hand.

"You'd prefer me to act otherwise?" she countered, batting those lush auburn lashes at me. "Because I'll happily scream, if that would make you feel better."

My lips curled. "Oh, I would enjoy that, but perhaps in the bedroom later. Not here." I pulled her forward before she could reply, but didn't miss the small gasp in my wake. She probably expected me to finish what we started at *Diavolo Rojo*. As much as I would enjoy that, I really needed a fucking nap. I'd wanted one on the train but didn't trust her not to try something while I slept.

The hotel I'd booked near the meet-up spot would have to do.

Movement in my peripheral vision had my lips inching upward.

Amara didn't flinch, her expression artfully blank, her posture sure.

But she'd just swiped a knife from a table as we passed a coffee shop. I caught the flash of metal as it disappeared into her hand.

I hid a smile, amused.

She could keep the butter knife.

Maybe we'd even play with it later. Then I'd introduce her to one of the daggers hidden beneath my clothes, teach her what a blade really felt like against her delicate skin.

I led her away from the stream of human traffic toward the garage, anticipating her strike. But it never came. Not even when we found the car I'd procured. If anything, she appeared too busy gaping at the beautiful sports car— black, of course—with a leather interior and a manual transmission.

"Get in," I demanded, holding the passenger-side door open for her.

She shrugged and slid into the bucket seat, the knife nowhere to be seen. I suspected she hid it up the sleeve of her brown jacket or maybe in the pocket of her jeans.

If she planned to stab me while driving, we'd have a problem. Not that it would work—a blunt edge like that would bruise more easily than slice through my clothes. Still, it would suck.

I dropped her bag in the trunk in the front of the car, debating if I wanted to say anything. As she seemed content to stare out the window, seat belt already buckled,

I decided against it and settled beside her instead.

She appeared to be waiting, so I'd wait with her.

And in the meantime, I'd acquaint myself with my new toy. Temporary, likely, but fun.

The engine roared to life, causing me to grin. Amara shifted subtly, her gaze flashing to the dashboard, eyeing the interlocking-ring symbol on the steering wheel and returning her focus to the parking garage.

I snorted. She might not find the fine piece of German machinery gorgeous, but I certainly did. And I particularly enjoyed the way it rumbled beneath me as I pulled out of the parking spot to head toward the exit.

Amara didn't perk up until I entered the highway system, her intrigue palpable as I was finally allowed to drive the car as intended.

And I did.

I floored it to the speed of my desire, flying past others on the Autobahn with ease and loving the hell out of the Audi R8. It was really too fucking bad that we couldn't drive like this in the United States. Of course, it didn't stop me from trying, but the liberty of not having to worry about any trouble put me at ease in a way I couldn't experience back home.

Not that I did a lot of driving in New Orleans or New York City—my two primary residences.

"My father owned a car like this," Amara said quietly, her voice thoughtful. "I always thought it was wasted on him."

"You mean Geoff Rose?" I asked, recalling the records I found about her adoption.

The Rose family had taken her in at the age of seven, providing her with a life that most orphans dreamed about. Which made her choice of profession a bit confusing. She didn't need money. But maybe she enjoyed playing with the country's elite? I could understand that on a level. I became a Cavalieri for a similar reason.

"Yeah," she replied. "Daddy Rose."

"He's in Maine, right?"

She shrugged. "Honestly? I have no idea. He and Clarissa move a lot."

"Clarissa?" I repeated.

"Yeah. My, uh, mom."

She calls her adoptive mother by her first name? Interesting.

"Anyway, the nature of their business takes them wherever their client desires," she continued, her attention on the sights outside. "Whatever the recent trends are, they study them, learn them, cater to them. And they constantly run the auction circuit. So." She shrugged again. "Their whereabouts are usually unknown."

"Auction circuit?" I asked, frowning.

"Girls, Killian." She glanced at me sideways. "Girls like me."

AMARA

I didn't know why I admitted that to him. But his assumptions about me being a con artist pissed me off. At least it confirmed he wasn't one of Malcom's goons. They were all very well aware of my former fiancé's proclivities.

And definitely familiar with the auction scene.

I shivered, folding into myself on the seat. "When are we meeting Boris?" I asked, needing to know how many minutes I had left.

"Boris?"

"Malcom's right-hand man." I had no doubt that monster would be the one picking me up. And he'd likely welcome me back into the fold using one of his favorite methods as well. My mouth flattened at the thought, my throat already threatening to gag.

That man would choke me to death if Malcom let him.

Maybe this time he would.

A treacherous tear threatened to fall, but I flicked it away before Killian could see. Not that I entirely cared if he knew how I felt. More that I didn't want to show weakness with him, or anyone.

"Tonight," he replied, his voice flat. "And Malcom didn't mention a Boris."

"He'll be there." With a few of his minions. The evening would be fun. Maybe they'd knock me out again so I wouldn't remember it all.

I'd managed to snag a knife on our walk through the station, but I knew it wouldn't help me. It'd been a quick thought, a hope underlined in stupidity. Killian had at least one real blade on him, likely more. Maybe even a gun.

And I had a fucking butter knife.

I almost wanted to laugh at how quickly he'd turned my world upside down, but I couldn't even blame him. This was all Malcom's fault. My parents', too.

Fuck, they weren't even my parents, but it was ingrained in me to think of them that way. A habit formed after years and years of calling them *Mom* and *Dad* in public, using their last name as my own, and pretending to be from their wealthy, sick world.

My real parents, the ones who actually created me, had sold me at the age of seven to be groomed for an auction.

But I'd been deemed special.

Unique.

Intelligent.

And so the Rose family had kept me, grooming me with homeschooling before sending me to one of the finest academic institutions for college, therefore ensuring I would have the appropriate background for a high-society client. A perfect lady in public, a deviant in the bedroom. Trained to seduce men for information while maintaining a charade as a submissive housewife.

Hell.

That was how I described it.

I started plotting my escape the night I met Malcom. The night he acquired me. The night he fucked me and then gave me to his associates for fun. To watch. To see how much I could endure until I cried.

But I knew too much for a man like Malcom to just let me disappear. It wasn't about pride or money. It was about the conversations I'd overheard. The details he'd tasked me with learning.

I knew everything.

His plans.

His intended future.

His business associates—several of which were illegal.

And most importantly, I knew about his ties to Amir.

Just thinking of the name sent a chill down my spine. That man oozed evil intent. I feared him more than I feared Malcom.

Was that who he would give me to? The vile male had always wanted a piece of me, but Malcom never allowed it, too covetous of his prize. Amir's proclivities ran much darker than Malcom's. I wouldn't survive his brand of pleasure.

Swallowing the bile rising in my throat, I focused on our surroundings, on the powerful car rumbling beneath me.

There's still time, I promised myself. *You got away once. You can do it again.*

But I was so tired. I hadn't slept in over twenty-four hours. Not necessarily a new habit for me, but the lack of adrenaline fueling my movements caused the exhaustion to seduce me like a long-lost mistress.

Perhaps a nap was a good idea. It wasn't like I could escape Killian while he drove, especially not at these speeds.

The odd cuff held me captive as well. Resting seemed appropriate. Maybe I could catch him off guard when we stopped, after I'd recouped some much-needed energy.

A solid plan.

For now.

Ugh, too hot.

I kicked the blankets from my legs, thankful for the cool air that touched my bare skin, and sighed. So much better. Now I could sleep.

Something about that nagged at my mind, my dream-induced state foggy.

I shook it off, needing more rest. Every part of me felt weighed down, exhausted, as if I hadn't slept in years. Or was waking from a serious hangover.

Did I drink last night?

No.

Wait…

My eyes flew open, taking in the unfamiliar surroundings of the too-dark room. Curtains had been drawn over the windows, hiding the time of day. But the clock on the nightstand showed it was nearing the evening hours.

And the man on the bed beside me brought everything back in a whirl.

Killian Bedivere.

An assassin for hire who meant to take me back to Malcom.

An assassin who had fallen asleep.

He actually appeared quite peaceful, in a beautiful sort of way, with his thick, dark hair swept to the side, his defined cheekbones relaxed. That jaw was still as chiseled as ever, and damn, he still wore a shirt. Granted, the white fabric clung to his muscles, accentuating strong arms lying loose at his sides.

Huh.

I glanced around, disturbed that he'd somehow managed to get me up here without me waking.

Even more disturbed to find that he'd removed my boots, jeans, and jacket, leaving me in a tank top, a bra, and a thong.

My guardians always said I could sleep through a tornado. They weren't wrong, especially when I went too long without any rest, and I'd been constantly moving for weeks. Strange that I chose Killian's presence to finally relax in—strange *and* stupid.

Where did he put my jeans? The room appeared spotless, my clothing and bag nowhere to be seen. Maybe they were in the bathroom?

As silently as possible, I crept out of the bed to tiptoe into the en-suite bathroom, my gaze widening at the elegant furnishings. This was definitely not a cheap motel. The walk-in marble shower, double sink, and heated floors suggested wealth and opulence, especially for a European hotel.

And, of course, the room was completely empty.

Where did you hide my stuff?

I sighed, eyeing the cuff on my wrist and then my reflection in the mirror. A glimmer of hopelessness stared back at me. The expression of a woman on the edge of defeat.

How could I escape? He even had that stupid butter knife.

My shoulders fell, my options swimming out of reach, leaving me in the deep end to drown.

After all that planning, my only chance at running was gone. Destroyed by a man I hardly knew who had bested me mere hours after meeting.

I wasn't weak.

But he made me feel inferior, as if I stood no chance to survive.

Because I don't.

The glassy glimmer in my gaze had me cringing. This wasn't me. I didn't give up. I fought. I just didn't know how. He'd cornered me in a way few others ever had. All for Malcom. That made Killian one of the bad guys by association.

I have to fight him.

We'd played before.

This wouldn't be a game. This would be real. It was my only shot.

Steeling my spine, I glowered at the meek female in the mirror. I'd rather die than go back to Malcom. And if that meant provoking Killian into killing me, so be it. Dying by his hand would be far better than returning to the hell I'd escaped from.

He thought I was a con artist. Assumed that meant I deserved this fate. Fine. I'd play that to my advantage. Push him into hurting me. Fighting. Maybe I could grab a blade off him. Or a gun.

The idea had me slipping back into the bedroom. He hadn't moved, his chest rising and falling softly in a pattern of sleep.

Where's your jacket? I wondered, scanning the two chairs and the couch, my gaze finally landing on the closet across from his bed.

Bull's-eye.

I crept forward on silent feet and jostled the door. It opened with a soft snick that had me glancing over my shoulder. Killian took a deep breath but otherwise remained still.

Good.

Okay.

Pulling open the door, I eyed his jacket hanging inside and frowned at the empty space. No sign of my belongings, but maybe his pockets held something of interest.

Sure enough, a dagger rested inside an interior compartment. Small, but sharp. It fit in the palm of my hand easily.

This was much better than the butter knife.

And I had the advantage with him being passed out.

Oh, but first, I needed that device. Which, of course, wasn't in his coat. It had to be on him somewhere. I could find it after I took care of him.

My heart skipped a beat, the notion of taking his life not appealing. He wouldn't be the first, but that didn't make this any easier.

Remember your training, I thought with a breath. *You can do this.*

Sweat trickled across my brow, the heat of the room seeming to swarm around me, causing my steps to slow as I neared him. The two times Malcom made me kill for him, I'd poisoned my victims post-sex. They told me what my master needed to know, and I rewarded them by slipping a lethal concoction into their drinks.

I hated myself for it.

Hated Malcom, too.

Hated this *life.*

And here I was, about to kill for a third time. Not because he made me do it, but because I had no other alternative. I couldn't go back to Malcom. I knew what he would do to me, the scum he'd sell me to, and recognized what my future would become.

I lifted the knife, aiming for his neck, knowing it would be the quickest way to incapacitate him. But I hesitated. My hand literally froze inches from his neck, my conscience perking up her ugly head and screaming at me about right and wrong.

He's one of them, I told myself. *He's working for Malcom.*

My resolve wavered, my grip tightening, my need to escape pushing at me for freedom.

One swipe. That's all. A quick cut across his throat. It's not hard. Just move. I bit my lip, stealing a deep breath through my nose. *Now or never.*

I swung, my limbs shaking, only to have the world shift from under my feet. A shriek left my lips as I landed hard against the mattress, Killian on top of me with the blade pressed to my throat. My wrist burned from whatever twist he'd done to dislodge the weapon from my hand, his chest hard against mine, one of his thighs pinning me to the mattress.

He tsked. "Oh, sweet Amara. When you hesitated, I thought you might care." The metal kissed my neck, causing me to shiver. "Rule number one: never turn a dagger on someone who knows how to use it better than you do." He slid the knife menacingly across my skin, leaving a sting in its wake. "Rule number two: always follow through. Hesitation is what will get you killed."

His words shattered the last vestiges of will I had inside me.

I'll never break free of him.

"You win," I whispered, exhausted.

"Darling, I won the moment I found you." He trailed the knife downward, slicing through the cotton of my tank top with expert ease. He made it look so simple, as if he did this every day. And maybe he did. However, cutting clothing like that took skill, something he clearly possessed.

I squirmed, the caress of lethal steel against my skin leaving me hot and cold beneath him.

"This is pretty," he murmured, drawing the tip of his knife over the swell of my breast as my chest rose and fell in quick succession. "If we had more time, I'd pick up where we left off in the club."

Meaning we were meeting Malcom's men soon.

My throat went dry, my hands curling into fists.

If I fought Killian, maybe he'd kill me. That had to be a better fate than what lay ahead. But did—

I hissed as he pressed the blade to my nipple through the thin lace of my black bra, the sharp point pricking my sensitive skin. His palm landed on my sternum, holding me down as I instinctively arched into him.

"Careful, kitten," he murmured, his opposite hand still holding the knife against my breast. "I'll draw blood when I want to, not because you're forcing me to."

I shivered, confused by the prickle of desire rushing through me at his words and the touch that followed. The palm against my sternum moved to my throat while his opposite hand drifted downward, dragging the knife along my skin to the lace of my panties. A twist of his wrist had the band snapping at the side, leaving my hip exposed to his blade.

"Killian," I whispered, uncertain of his intentions. This was different from the club, where I maintained control, or at least the pretense of it.

But this...

Killian owned every second, every breath. I had no choice here, no ability to deny or consent to anything he wanted to do.

I was quite literally his to play with as he saw fit.

And for some dark, fucked-up reason, that left me craving more.

I *wanted* him to take away my choice, to give me a moment of peace without thought, to steal me from this hellish reality and give me something *real*.

It unnerved me, accelerated my breath, caused my heart to speed up, and forced my lips to part.

Every male of my past had been one of someone else's choosing. Never mine. And for the first time in my life, I found myself actually desiring one. Albeit, the wrong one, but I wanted him all the same.

His lips curled at the sides, his thigh shifting away from mine. He balanced on his side, his grip around my throat tightening, his gaze holding mine. "Have you ever taken a life, Amara?"

I swallowed, his palm constricting the movement. "Yes."

He tilted his head to the side, the blade sliding beneath the lace along my shaved mound. "Yet you hesitated."

"Yes," I repeated.

"Why?"

I didn't want to answer that, so I merely stared back at him.

Which caused him to grin in response. "I do love the fire in you." The metal skimmed my sensitive skin, dipping between my thighs.

My limbs locked, my breath freezing in my lungs.

"Try not to move," he murmured. "I would hate to

harm such a pretty cunt." The tip of the blade met my clit, causing my hands to fist, my heart to race. Not in fear, but in excitement.

Men had done a lot of things to me over the years, but this... this was new.

He held my gaze, his pupils expanding as he slipped the dagger deeper, parting my slick folds in the most lethal of ways.

I shouldn't like this.

This is wrong.

Yet the inability to move, to push against the blade for friction, nearly killed me. And his smile said he knew it.

"Beautiful, Amara," he whispered, the steel gliding through my arousal.

I whimpered as the sensation disappeared, craving more even though I shouldn't. This dominant man had a hold on me I couldn't explain. He provided a mental escape that I needed, one that left me helpless and wanting beneath him.

And also shaking with an uncontrollable need.

"Part those pretty lips for me," he coaxed, pressing the sharp tip to the edge of my mouth as he shifted his hold to the side of my neck.

My eyes widened even as I complied, my pulse thundering in my ears. *What is he going to do? Was this all a way to toy with me before death? To leave me wanting in the worst possible way before taking my life?*

"Stay very still." The words were so low, the timbre of his voice stroking me in all the right places.

Warm, damp steel slid across my lips, a familiar musky essence coating my mouth.

Oh, fuck...

My thighs clenched, my nipples hardening to painful points. He'd literally seduced me with a dagger. This man I hardly knew, this assassin sent to retrieve me, had me panting beneath his hands after a few mere strokes of his blade.

And as he leaned down to taste me, sliding the knife back to my throat, I gave in to him.

His tongue traced my lips, setting off a flurry of sensations in my lower belly. A low growl emanated from his chest, vibrating the air between us and causing me to writhe in want. "Fuck, you're delicious, Amara. So damn delicious." He deepened the kiss, my arousal heightening the flavors between us as he memorized every inch of my mouth.

It felt like a claiming.

A vow.

A binding between us of a future cemented in blood.

Which was impossible because I knew his intentions for me, and yet my fingers clutched his shoulders, holding him to me. He devoured me in response, the jagged edge at my throat unmoving.

It was the perfect dichotomy of fire and ice. With one touch, he heated me from the inside out while the knife remained cold and threatening against my skin.

I wanted to moan. To scream. To plead with him to do *something*, anything other than continue to torture me in this way.

While a small voice in the back of my head screamed at me to fight.

I was paralyzed, unable to make a choice, my heart, mind, and body completely at odds with one another. The intoxicating blend left me light-headed, sending me to a place of existence where I could no longer care, where I just needed to feel.

He pulled back, his eyes glazed with desire, his mouth curled in amusement. "I'm so damn tempted to keep you." He brushed his lips over mine. "But I can't. You're the job, darling. And as I already told you, I don't fail."

His mouth met mine again, the pacing different, more intense, harsh, oddly fulfilling.

My tongue battled his, memorizing our mutual attraction. I'd never been with a man I actually wanted, and while I definitely should not desire this man, I did. Kissing him was not a chore but a luxury.

An excitement I'd never before experienced, one that ended too soon with him pulling away, the knife disappearing with his heat.

I blinked up at him, panting for more.

He ran his hand through his dark hair and then over his face, blowing out a breath and shaking his head as he rolled off the bed. "You need to get dressed. We're going to be late."

KILLIAN

I shouldn't have done that.

I knew better.

Rule number one: never fall for the mark.

And fuck if I wanted to break rule number one right now. Damn, twenty minutes later and I could still taste her on my tongue.

This savage need to take her was dangerous and overwhelming my ability to think clearly. Part of me wanted to keep her. An insane idea. It would end up being temporary with me eventually returning her to Senator Jenkins, or maybe letting her go, but it completely broke protocol.

I did not break the rules of engagement for anyone. I always delivered my marks, dead or alive, and I never faltered.

So why her? What was different about Amara?

She sat absolutely still beside me in the car, wearing her jeans and boots and a new tank top from her bag—all items I'd hidden from her in the room.

No butter knife. I threw that cheap weapon knockoff in the trash.

Not that she would know how to use it anyway. The way she'd held my blade—a real one that could actually do harm—showcased her rookie skills. Yet, she hadn't blinked an eye when I asked if she'd killed before. She never explained why she hesitated with me, but something told me it was more than her not knowing how to properly wield a blade. I'd seen the regret in her eyes, battling the strength and will to survive.

Her terror of being returned to Senator Jenkins went far deeper than a con woman fearing punishment for her crimes. Something here wasn't adding up. She mentioned auctions, suggesting she'd been sold in one. It could all be a clever ruse, but I read people for a living. And Amara didn't exude any hints of a lie in her words. Her actions also indicated the potential truth of her claim.

I mingled with politicians, billionaires, business tycoons, and celebrities, but I refrained from involving myself in the darker aspects of high society.

Auctions were a normal occurrence, a way to throw money around while feeling charitable for a good cause.

But that was not that realm Amara spoke of when she provided that detail from her past.

Her words had suggested a trafficking ring of sorts, which I knew existed. Buying slaves dated back to early civilization, and while there were laws against it now, money trumped reason. There were some sick fucks in this world. I'd met several through my line of work, had enjoyed killing a few of them, too.

And now it seemed the famous senator was involved in some nefarious activities. An interesting accusation, one that could derail his plans for the future.

The public adored him, many wanting him to run in the next presidential election despite his young age of thirty-six. If Amara's words were proven true, she could destroy his entire career.

Which also gave him cause to silence her.

Yet, he wanted her alive. Why?

She appeared to have given up beside me, her shoulders slumped, her gaze on the dark sky beyond. Jenkins's meeting was located away from the city, in a rural area with minimal people. I assumed he chose it in case she decided to run again, but her body language told me she had no intention of sneaking off this time. She knew I had her and there wasn't anything she could do about it.

Amara had accepted her fate.

That usually thrilled me, the chase complete. But her defeat didn't excite me at all. It actually made me want to turn the car around and take her far away from Jenkins's men.

This attraction was fucking with my head. Kissing her had been a huge mistake. I hadn't meant to, but she'd triggered my darker inclinations when she tried to slice my throat. Taunting her with the knife came naturally, her responding arousal heightening the moment and pushing me further into this deadly game between us.

Fuck, I wanted more. So much more.

She's not mine.

She could be.

Mission first.

Fuck the mission.

The conflicting thoughts harassed me all the way to our meeting place. Amara stiffened as we entered one of the various industrial areas of Solar Valley, tugging her lip between her teeth.

A myriad of words caught on my tongue, most of them an apology for what was about to happen, confusing the hell out of me. I never apologized. Ever. My marks always deserved their fates, but I couldn't fight the inkling that perhaps Amara didn't deserve hers.

Shoving the concerns from my head, I focused on our surroundings, searching for Jenkins's men.

Distractions were dangerous.

Amara was dangerous.

Four vehicles were parked up ahead, all SUVs, with over a dozen men standing outside of them with casual stances.

Too casual.

I frowned as we approached, red flags waving in my head. "Does your betrothed typically guard you with an army?"

She shrugged. "I had a few bodyguards."

"How many?" I pressed.

"Three." She glanced at me. "Why?"

I didn't reply, eyeing the scene before us. All of them were armed. Some more than others. And two more cars were parked behind them, with a handful of men spread out along the main road.

At least twenty goons, all trying too hard to look casual.

"Do you recognize any of them, Amara?" I asked as we parked about thirty feet away from the troop in front of us. They had formed a U-shaped perimeter with our position being at one end.

"Unfortunately," she muttered, her hand already on the door.

I reached over to stop her. "Who do you recognize?"

She blew out a breath, her gaze snagging on the one in the middle. "That's Boris. The rest..." She shrugged. "He likes his goons."

"But does he usually send this many?"

Her gaze finally met mine. "No. Why?"

"Because I find it rather odd that your dear senator has sent a welcoming caravan of twenty men to restrain one woman."

She smirked in reply, shaking her head. "It's probably his version of a punishment. Maybe they'll let you join, finish what we started earlier."

The cold words froze me inside. "You think he's..." I couldn't even finish that thought or statement, my blood boiling so hot it resembled ice.

"It wouldn't be the first time," she replied, sounding so detached my heart hurt. "Well, maybe with twenty. It's usually four, maybe five. But I've pissed him off. So." Another shrug, as if this type of treatment were the most normal thing in the world to her.

"That's why you ran," I realized, and the look she gave me confirmed it. Oh, this could all be an act, but I knew a broken soul when I saw one. And it was staring me back in the face now, all of her defenses gone.

Because she'd given up.

Fuck.

A shuffle in front of me had my gaze snapping to the men, my jaw tensing.

No. She might be right about a punishment, but there was something else at play here. I could practically taste the adrenaline on my tongue, the impending fight, the excitement in the air.

Amara was their dessert, not their entrée.

I gave them all a little wave, feigning a calm I didn't feel, and leaned over to pull a box from a compartment behind Amara's seat. All my cars came equipped with a small rectangular container, as per my arrangement with the consulting agency I went through.

Pressing my thumb to the sensor along the edge caused the case to open with a hiss.

A pistol with two magazines sat waiting for me inside. I tucked them into my jacket, the darkness of our interior hiding my actions from the observers outside. It helped that I'd left the high beams on, illuminating and blinding them all.

I added two flash bangs to my pockets, along with two daggers, and plucked a pair of earplugs from the pile as well.

"Follow my lead," I told Amara, killing the engine but not the lights. I returned the box to its rightful place while she watched.

"Not like I have a choice, right?" she countered, her voice flat. Cold. She'd already turned herself off, displaying a woman I barely recognized. Not that I really knew her, but this was not the female I tracked down at the bar but a girl beaten down to a point of surrender.

If this was all an act, I'd kill her myself.

But I trusted my instincts and abilities. They'd served me well thus far.

I put the plugs in my ears, well versed in reading lips in my profession. "Let's go." I didn't wait for her to comply, just stepped out of the car, the remote to her cuff a calming weight in my hand as I nudged the door closed with my opposite palm.

"Gentlemen," I greeted, purposely standing to the side of the car where I'd blend into the shadows lurking beyond the light. "I've got to tell you, this little firecracker is a handful." I peered into the center of the mass, identifying the one Amara had recognized. "Boris, right?"

A hint of annoyance flashed over his features, his lips moving to form the words, "I see she's been talking."

"She wouldn't shut up." I infused a hint of irritation into my tone while I spoke. "I'll be very glad to get this trade over with."

Boris nodded. "Excellent. Come here, Amara."

She didn't move, defiance written all over her stance. Or perhaps she noticed what I did about the eager men dotting the perimeter.

They weren't staring at her with hungry eyes, but at me.

Clear rookies from their inabilities to hide their intentions.

This is definitely an ambush. And Jenkins hadn't been thorough enough to send qualified assassins to take me out. Instead he'd employed roughly two dozen untrained men. The only one who appeared at ease was Boris, the obvious leader.

He would be the one I needed to take down first.

"Hold on. Before I send her over, I need to know if you want the cuff or not."

Boris gazed in my general direction, his men antsy at his back. "Cuff?"

"Yeah, it's how I tagged her. Sort of like a fancy shock collar that doubles as a GPS tracking device. You can test it if you want." I left the offer hanging, my tone nonchalant. When he didn't reply, I shrugged. "Well, it's worth too much to go to waste, so if you don't want it, I'll just take it back, then." I started backward, toward the rear of the car, my eyes on his mouth.

"Wait," he said, causing my lips to curl. "A shock collar?" Even from thirty feet away, I could see the evil intent pouring from his stance and expression. "Can it go around her neck?"

I chuckled. "Nah, it's designed for the wrist. It's perfect for bringing a woman to her knees without risking her throat."

Amara gasped while Boris smiled. "Yeah, I'll test that"

was his reply.

"It's a lot of fun," I said. I moved in front of the car, standing directly in the center of the headlights.

Now would be the correct time to shoot me, except they were all awaiting their leader's signal. And I'd intrigued the man in charge too much for him to act.

I held up my hand, showing the remote. "Catch." I tossed it to him, my aim true just like with my daggers, and he caught it in his palm. "You just have to hit the button," I explained, tucking my hands into my pockets to find the flash bangs.

"Step into the light, Amara," Boris urged, a vicious grin spreading over his lips. "You know how much I've missed you. And Malcom's given me permission to play."

She didn't move.

"Now, Amara," I added, my tone laced with command. I didn't chance a glance at her but felt her gaze on me.

And then heard her boots shuffling against the gravel.

Good girl, I thought as she moved to my side, her expression stoic.

I took a subtle step forward, not wanting her within touching distance.

"This button?" Boris asked, his thumb hovering over

the only trigger on the device.

"Yep," I replied, my own thumbs pressing down on the items in my hands.

His forearm flexed, giving me the signal to close my eyes and toss the flash bangs to the side.

Boom!

The crack ricocheted around us, the light bright behind my closed eyes.

But I'd been the only one prepared, the earplugs saving my hearing and keeping me upright while everyone else reacted.

I analyzed the scene in quick succession, my pistol already in my hand and taking aim.

Seven to the left. *Bang. Bull's-eye. Bang. Forehead. Refocus. Bang. Bang. Headshot.* Seven down.

An eighth bullet went dead center, taking out the man directly beside a screaming Boris. I left him alone, switching out my magazine in two beats, then took out six more men along the sides.

A bullet whizzed by my head, causing me to tuck and roll to the side, finding the closest meat-shield to eat the incoming fire. He was already dead, having met my fatal mark first, and absorbed the impact as I picked off two more of the men. Not having a free hand to replenish my gun, I threw a blade into a heaving chest before bending to retrieve Victim One's gun.

Fully loaded machine pistol—perfect.

With him as my armor, I took out the remaining assholes along the periphery.

Silence met my execution, Amara cowering beside the vehicle, her eyes wide.

I removed my earplugs, pocketing them. "Don't move," I told her, making my way toward Boris. He seemed to be missing a hand, courtesy of the remote.

And wouldn't you know? The cocky bastard wasn't even armed, having relied on all his men to protect him with their street-purchased weapons.

Poor form, really.

This entire job had been a fuckup from the moment it had started.

He groaned, his good arm wrapped around the damaged one.

"I'm sorry. Did I forget to mention that only my thumbprint can activate the device? My bad." It was a fail-safe should the intended mark ever steal the gadget from my grasp. Or in this case, an asshat. "So what was the plan here? Take the girl back and kill me?"

"F-fuck you," he spat, cradling his stubby arm against his blood-soaked chest.

"Ah, I think you meant that for Amara, who, by the way, will never be touched by you again." I pressed my boot to his neck. "Now I'm going to ask you again. What was the plan here?"

He sputtered another expletive that had me tsking.

"Perhaps you're not hearing me." I released his neck to crouch down beside him, a blade slipping into my hand. "I just took out nearly two dozen of your men in less than twenty seconds."

"You're insane!" he yelled.

"You would not be the first to level that accusation at me. But I have to ask, who is more insane in this situation? Me for defending myself, or you for thinking you and your men had a chance against me?"

He growled, fury causing his nostrils to flare.

"I didn't catch that, Boris. Was that supposed to be an explanation of sorts?" I pressed the blade to his inner thigh, slicing right through his black jeans to meet his skin. "Or do you need an incentive to start talking?"

I punctuated the point against the side of his balls,

eliciting a shriek from him just as his pocket began to vibrate.

"Ah, I wonder who that could be." I fished the phone out to eye the name on the display.

"You're going to play along, Boris." I settled the knife against him. "Or you'll lose your sack."

He grimaced.

"Say *yes*," I told him, my finger hovering over the Accept button.

"Yessss," he hissed, his black eyes blazing with a mix of rage and terror.

He was totally going to botch this up, but that was what I wanted.

I selected the Speaker button, saying nothing.

"Is it done?" a sharp voice asked. One that matched the name on the ID—Senator Malcom Jenkins.

I cocked a brow at Boris, who seemed to be struggling to make a decision.

The crinkle of his brow alerted me to his choice before the words started spilling from his mouth. "He took out all—"

I sliced through his groin with a shake of my head and sighed. "That's not what we agreed upon, Boris," I said, wiping my blade on his thigh and enjoying his gurgling screams. They truly set the tone for the conversation to come.

I stood, switching off the speakerphone and pressing the device to my ear. "Really, Senator, you need to pay for better help."

"Mister Bedivere," he replied, his tone surprised. "I'm confused. Has something happened?"

"I don't know, Senator. You tell me." Because the last time I checked, he was supposed to send payment in exchange for his runaway bride. Not send a horde of amateurs to take me out.

A beat of silence followed. "I... I'm sorry, but you have me at a loss. I sent my emissaries to retrieve Amara. Is she all right?"

Ah, so that was how he wanted to play it? "Your former fiancée is fine. Your men, however, are not."

"Has she done something?" he asked, his voice hardening.

"Amara? No. She's feisty but harmless." *Unless equipped with a syringe of ketamine.*

He cleared his throat. "Look, Killian. I don't know what she's said to you, but she's a master manipulator.

Don't make the mistake of listening to her. Everything she'll tell you is a lie."

My eyebrows rose. "Is that what this is about, then? Why you considered me a loose end?" It was the only explanation I could draw from him sending this many men to take me down.

"A loose end?" He actually laughed, the sound smooth. Too smooth. "Is that what she has you believing?"

I smiled, amused. His deception was flawless. If his emissaries hadn't been packing hardcore artillery, I might have been tempted to believe him. But my instincts weren't wrong. He'd sent these men here to kill me, not her.

"Oh, she's gotten to you," he continued, sighing. "I'm so sorry, Killian. She is quite good, though. She played me as well. We can still work this out, you and I."

"Yeah? What's she worth to you?" I asked, curious.

"I'll double the reward on her head," he said immediately.

I whistled. "Well, that is an impressive offer. But we still have a problem."

"Whatever it is, I can fix it."

"Can you?" I countered. "Because I have to say, fucking with a Cavalieri was not one of your wisest decisions.

However, I do have a suggestion, if you're interested."

"Name it." He sounded so sure of himself, as if trying to have me killed was an everyday business deal. *Righteous prick.*

"Next time? Send an army. A trained one."

Movement in my peripheral vision had me hanging up the phone and switching focus. I dropped the device and moved toward the nearest dead body to retrieve a gun, then aimed for the path beside Amara's fleeing feet.

She froze, the bullet barely missing her leg. "The next one goes in your calf, Amara," I called to her. "Now get in the fucking car."

Because she had a hell of a lot of explaining to do.

A man like Jenkins didn't send a group of thugs to retrieve a runaway con-artist bride. And he certainly didn't risk pissing off the head of the Tabella Della Morte by taking out one of his assassins with a shitty hit.

No, there was something far more pressing happening here. She'd mentioned the auctions, suggesting he'd bought her at one. Fine. That was damning evidence, but still her word against his.

Which told me that little truth was only the tip of the iceberg.

Amara knew something far more deadly to the senator's reputation. Something important enough for him to try to kill me just for having spent some time with her.

I sent a bullet into Boris's skull before tossing the gun to the ground.

This place needed a cleanup crew. Stat.

Pulling out my own phone, I sent a text to the team lead who handled these issues. I included a set of coordinates and the number of casualties. They had contacts all over the world on standby specifically to address these types of situations.

Out of the corner of my eye, I watched as Amara slid into the passenger seat. The high beams made it impossible to see her inside, but I suspected she would be trying to get into my weapons stash right about now.

Good luck, sweetheart. There were two containers, both of which would only open for my fingerprint. *Gotta love technology.*

I was also surrounded by an array of discarded firearms, most of which were actually quite impressive. They'd make good gifts for the cleanup crew.

The straightening of her shoulders as I approached the driver's side confirmed my suspicions.

"Fighting me right now would not be a smart move, Amara," I warned as I settled beside her. Adrenaline pumped headily through my veins, my killing drive still raging inside me.

She froze beside me, fear wafting off her in waves. She could probably taste the lethal energy fueling my every move, a side effect of having just taken down nearly two dozen men. It left me feeling alive, indestructible, and furious.

Jenkins had thought me so inept that his little horde of incompetent soldiers could take me down? It was fucking insulting.

I reversed the Audi down the long drive, the growl of the engine matching the one in my chest.

Peeling out at the end of the road, I sent us flying forward toward the Autobahn.

And then a ringing sang through the car's system.

I knew who it was without looking, hitting the Accept button. "Arthur."

"What the fuck are you doing, Dagger? Senator Jenkins just called claiming you've lost your mind over a girl."

I snorted. "I bet he did." My grip tightened on the steering wheel. "Did he happen to mention the greeting party he sent to the meeting spot?"

"Yes. He claims you killed them all."

"I did."

"Why?" he demanded.

"There were roughly two dozen heavily armed men waiting for the delivery. What does that tell you?"

He remained quiet for a moment, then replied, "Seems a bit much for one girl."

"My thoughts exactly," I muttered.

More silence.

Arthur Calthorpe was a lot of things—cold, unapologetic, sadistic. But he trusted his Cavalieri implicitly.

I had no reason to lie to him. Not now, not ever. I always completed my jobs on time or early, and earned him several bonuses throughout the years.

Reliable was my middle name.

I did not fuck up.

And he knew it.

"Find out what she knows," he finally said, hanging up, his order a new task.

He would expect me to go to whatever lengths were required to discern the truth.

Including torturing Amara.

"I hope you're ready to talk, kitten," I warned. "Or it's going to be a very long night."

AMARA

Killian killed all those men.

Without blinking an eye.

Shot at me with a precision that left me frozen midstep.

Every action measured, precise, revealing a predator before my eyes. Each bullet had sailed into the skull or chest of his victims, sending them to the pavement before they could even register what he'd done.

I watched it all from the ground, too stunned from the bombs he'd thrown to move. My ears were still ringing from the impact.

The angel of death beside me hadn't been affected at all. Danger oozed from his aura, flooding the car and scattering goose bumps down my arms.

Amir terrified me.

Malcom angered me.

Killian intrigued me.

It made no sense. I should be terrified, pleading for my life, begging him to leave me somewhere. It was partly why I tried to run, my body too damn conflicted for my own sanity. Because seeing him single-handedly take down all those men had melted me into a hot puddle of *need*. And the wrongness of it had sent me fleeing.

Only to have him stop me with an act that just turned me on more.

This is so fucked up.

He wanted me to talk, to tell him things I could never say out loud, and I had no doubt he would resort to torture if needed. Killian exuded a calm demeanor, but I'd seen the real him back there. A feral beast lurked beneath his elegant veneer.

I wanted to stroke him. To play. To lick every inch of him.

My thighs clenched at the thought, my abdomen churning. Maybe it was the energy of the moment, the residual effects post-battle, but I craved a bite of his animalistic nature. It would be dark and sinful and would very likely hurt. Yet I didn't care.

"Are you hungry?" he asked, his deep voice exciting me more.

"Yes," I whispered. *But not for food.*

"Good."

That one word left me so hot I almost moaned. Jesus, he'd messed me up in the worst way. Or perhaps it was the best way. I didn't know, but I needed to get a grip on myself.

He killed at least twenty men.

And Boris.

My lips curled at that last one. Death never bothered me, having been well acquainted with it all my life. But I'd never been one to *enjoy* it.

Until today.

All those assholes deserved their fates. Especially Boris. My only regret was the swiftness with which Killian had ended their lives.

I'd warned him that Malcom would betray him. Fortunately, Killian realized it in time and handled the situation.

Still, it shocked me. A broken part of me had just accepted that all those men were there to teach me a lesson. Sure, it was extreme. However, Malcom adored his punishments, and I'd definitely infuriated him by running off.

I shivered, recalling the dreaded day.

Our wedding day.

"Look at you, all dressed in white." Boris's silky drawl sent a chill down my spine.

I refused to acknowledge him. He might read the plan in my eyes, and then I'd be trapped with nowhere to go.

This had to work.

There was no other way.

Malcom was officially distracted, his duty to his ego greater than his duty to guard me. All of his political associates—the legal ones—were here today. He wouldn't make a violent scene with all those cameras and eyes on him.

And he'd be too busy saving face afterward to track me right away. It provided the perfect cover, the time I needed, to run.

"Did you hear me?" Boris demanded, his breath hot on the back of my neck as he wrapped his arm around my waist, yanking me backward. "A slut in white is my favorite, Amara. Do you think Malcom will allow me a little taste before the vows? Or do you think he'll share you tonight?"

Bile lined my throat. Malcom loved a good celebration. He no doubt had something vile planned with me being the centerpiece. Or maybe he'd bring in some of his other girls for playtime.

I didn't know.

Didn't care.

Because I'd be long gone before the festivities began.

"Boris." The familiar voice made me think of nails on a chalkboard. It haunted my existence, reminded me of a life I'd rather forget. "You need to leave her alone before someone sees. You can play later."

The woman who pretended to be my mother came to stand at my side, her gray eyes aging at the sides despite the copious amounts of Botox she received.

"Yeah, yeah." He bit the back of my neck before releasing me. "Be a good girl, Amara. Think of me."

I ignored him, knowing it would infuriate him. But one cool glance from Clarissa Rose sent his boots shuffling backward.

No one argued with the Madam. Not in this world.

"You shouldn't antagonize him," she chastised.

Yes, because existing was my fault. Instead of voicing my opinion, I merely smiled. "He likes it."

She smirked. "Probably true." She turned to face me, her blonde hair perfectly styled, as always. "You really have turned out perfectly, darling Amara. I couldn't be more proud."

I shook off the memory, a vision of Clarissa's bloody face vibrant in my thoughts. A fantasy I'd long coveted that had yet to become a reality. But one day, I'd kill her.

And her poor excuse of a husband, too.

"Are you going to behave for me, Amara?" Killian asked as he pulled off the highway toward what appeared to be a city.

"Where would I go?" I countered. I had no idea where we were, having lost consciousness for who knew how long on our drive out of Berlin.

"Not far," he assured me. "But if you cause a scene when we arrive, you will regret it."

"Threats seem pretty irrelevant at this point, don't you think?" I side-eyed him. "I mean, we both know you're already planning to torture me, Killian." Because I had no intention of *talking*, like he suggested. He thought he wanted to know, but he didn't. No one wanted to play in the knowledge of my mind.

He didn't deny it, navigating the streets with ease and pulling up in front of a building. Killian unbuckled himself and leaned into my personal space—an easy feat considering the small interior of the sports car.

"I do intend to torment you, Amara. Thoroughly," he whispered against my ear. "But I need something to eat first." He nipped my earlobe and grabbed a box from behind my seat.

There were two.

I knew because I'd tried to open them both while he was outside the car.

"Don't move, Amara," he said, opening his door to greet the approaching valet in fluent German.

I considered disobeying him and exiting the car, just to see what he'd do. But I decided not to push him. That dangerous aura hadn't abated in the slightest, which told me he was still in a killing mood. And while I wanted to play, I also didn't want to die.

He handed over the keys before grabbing my bag from the trunk and walked around to finally allow me out of the car. I followed mutely as he led me into the opulent lobby. He kept talking about food, yet this was a hotel. A fancy one.

"Hold this," he said, handing me the box. My bag hung from his shoulder.

A woman from the reception desk waved us over, but

he merely nodded at her as he lifted a phone to his ear.

"Wyatt, I need a favor" was his greeting. "Yeah, yeah, add it to my tab. I'm in one of your hotels in Leipzig. Can you get me a room under an alias?"

He paused, smirking.

"Fine, your *brother's* hotel. Can you help me or not?" He smiled at whatever the other man said in reply. "I'll text you the info."

He continued listening, his dimples appearing.

"You're a real dick, Mershano." He laughed then, shaking his head. "Yeah, consider it a date. Cheers."

He hung up the phone with another chuckle before typing out a message to his friend.

"Mershano?" I repeated softly, eyeing the giant *M* insignia engraved into the middle of the lobby floor. "Mershano Suites." I'd never stayed at one, but I knew of them.

"Yeah." He glanced at his phone, reading some sort of response. "Wyatt's a friend."

"That's the rebellious one, right?" I asked, somewhat familiar with the family, not because of the circuit I belonged to, but just because of the fame of their names. They owned one of the finest lines of luxury hotels in the world. "Isn't the older one about to get married? After a reality show or something?"

Killian actually looked surprised. "You follow that shit?"

"Yes. I was trained to." A requirement of my upbringing and status.

His smirk died. "We're going to discuss that at length."

I shrugged. That part of my history I could divulge. It was the details about Malcom that I didn't want to elaborate on. Ever.

His phone buzzed again, causing his lips to curl as he typed out a reply. "Room's ready." He cocked his head toward the desk, indicating he wanted me to follow him.

I did because I had nowhere else to go.

I also had no way of knowing if this damn cuff on my wrist still worked or not. He'd thrown the remote to Boris right before all the chaos. And from what I gathered, the thing blew up in Boris's hand.

My lips twitched. It'd been a clever play. If only I could have pulled that final trigger. That had to be therapeutic in a way—to end the lives of those who tormented me.

Like Clarissa.

And Geoff, although he never touched me. He just

oversaw my training.

And Malcom.

My teeth clenched, my need for vengeance strong.

Yet Killian wasn't on my list at all. I didn't want to hurt him. Not in the way I did the others, anyway. He'd kidnapped me, pulled a knife on me twice now, and forced me to follow him like a pet. I should hate him.

But I didn't. Not even close.

The conundrum gave me a headache, causing me to massage my temples while he spoke to the receptionist and gave her a name of *Cav Dagger*. When he handed her a passport from his jacket, I stopped listening.

This man operated in an entirely different league.

He thanked the woman as she handed him a set of keys, then gestured for me to lead the way to the elevator bank across the marble-floored lobby.

Fine. I'd give him a sight to watch, swaying my hips as I sauntered ahead of him. A dress would have been better, but his resulting chuckle told me the jeans worked just fine.

"Playing the role of seductress, kitten?" he asked, using the key to select the floor he wanted.

The doors closed around us, leaving me alone with the lethal man who had just taken down twenty-plus men without getting a shred of evidence on him.

I tilted my head back to admire his amused features. "I thought you wanted to eat something."

"Oh, I do." He allowed his focus to shift downward, trailing slowly over every inch of my body, the innuendo clear. "We'll be ordering room service."

"And then?" I prompted.

His lips curled, his smoldering brown irises lifting to meet my gaze. "And then, my darling Amara, we'll play."

I shivered, not out of fear but in anticipation.

Because I *wanted* to play with him.

Which made me very broken indeed.

KILLIAN

Amara sat on the couch in the suite with her legs tucked beneath her and an empty plate in her lap. She'd clearly been as hungry as me, finishing her food in record time. Or maybe she just wanted to move on to our next task.

Torture.

Which wasn't going to happen.

This woman had been through enough over the years, telling me that she would be mostly immune to my methods anyway.

We would go about this using a different approach. One she'd never expect.

Standing, I took her plate and walked over to the table beside the kitchen area, stacking it with the other empty platters. Wyatt had reserved top-level accommodations for our stay at his brother's fancy hotel chain—Mershano

123

Suites. I approved. Especially of the king-sized bed in the other room.

Amara gazed up at me, her expression blank. She'd already retreated into herself, a defense mechanism for someone used to being hurt by others.

My blood boiled at the thought of what she'd been through, how she'd so openly accepted the idea of those twenty men being there for her *punishment*.

Arthur wanted answers. As did I. But this would be done my way. Without the use of my blade.

I settled on the couch beside her, keeping about a foot of distance between us, and shifted to bring my ankle up to my opposite knee. She didn't flinch or move as I stretched out my arm along the back cushions, leaving my hand a few inches from her shoulder. Nor did she react as I angled myself toward her.

She merely held my gaze. Emotionless. Ready to begin.

"So you're familiar with my family." We'd hit the high points during our initial meeting at the club. "I'm an heir to the Bedivere Corp. fortune who generally maintains a low profile. I'm seen just enough at charity events to maintain my cover while being perceived as living off my family inheritance without having to work a day in my life."

Similar to my buddy Wyatt, actually. But he, too, had his secrets.

Which brought me to my next point.

"It's amazing what money can hide, don't you think?" I leaned over to pick up my coffee mug and took a sip. Amara hadn't wanted an after-dinner beverage.

"I stopped being amazed years ago," she replied, tilting her head. "Are you going to regale me with stories to inspire me to talk? Because that'll get boring quickly."

"You'd prefer we jump to the point?" I countered, setting down my coffee mug and pulling out one of my knives. "Start the party early?" I tsked and twirled my blade. "Just last night we discussed conversation as foreplay."

"Right. I forgot. You're a talker." She waved me onward. "Continue delaying the inevitable. I'll try to appear anxious for you as I await your true intent."

I smirked. "Oh, I really do like you, Amara."

She snorted in reply, saying nothing more.

I traded my dagger for the coffee. "Growing up in your brother's shadow has its advantages. While everyone focused on him taking over Bedivere Corp., I learned how to blend into the background of high society and seek out my own activities. Like martial arts training, boxing, wrestling, even fencing. My parents didn't think much of it, just gave me a bank account to fund my social life, and I used it accordingly."

A flicker of interest flared in her eyes, her expression otherwise unreadable.

"My parents took me to this benefit in New Orleans right after I turned eighteen. I'm sure you've attended the sort—a party where money is thrown around under the pretense of benefiting a charity, but it's really about throwing status and names around?"

She nodded. "Yes. I've attended several. Campaign benefits, too. Though, I doubt your experience was similar to mine."

I raised a brow. "Did you kill anyone?"

She gave me a look. "I wanted to, but no." Interesting reply, one I'd dig into later.

"I did. At the benefit in New Orleans, I mean."

She leaned forward. "Why?"

"I walked in on something I shouldn't have and didn't particularly like what I saw." I shrugged. "When the guy noticed me in the doorway, he made the mistake of threatening me with a knife. I used it against him."

Now I had her full attention. "What was he doing?"

"Beating a woman to death." I finished my coffee and set the mug aside. "I reacted without thinking. Then found out he hadn't been the only male in the room. That's how I met Arthur Calthorpe."

She frowned, clearly unfamiliar with the name. "That's the guy you were talking to on the phone?"

Guy. I nearly laughed. "He manages the Tabella Della Morte. I'm one of his Cavalieri."

"And that's a fancy term for bounty-hunter assassin?"

"I'm a knight of death, sweetheart. Cavalieri Della Morte. There's twelve of us. Thirteen including Arthur."

"So he, what, recruited you?" she guessed.

"More or less. He'd been watching the scene unfold from the shadows."

"And didn't think to help the woman?"

I chuckled. "Not Arthur's style. He's a sadistic son of a bitch. Fortunately for me, the man I killed was causing him some business troubles. He called it a favor, told me he'd clean up the mess, and then called me two weeks later with an assignment. It started as blackmail—he had photos of me at the scene. But he kept giving me assholes to kill, people who had done some sort of wrong, and ten years later, I'm still helping him."

I resented him a bit at first, but each case was a new bastard who deserved his fate. And now I couldn't imagine any other life. He used me when he needed me, let me live in peace otherwise. A symbiotic relationship that allowed me to utilize and refine my skills in a lucrative manner.

"How many people have you killed?" she asked, not at all taken aback by my career path.

"More than I care to count," I admitted. "But I have one rule—the person has to deserve his or her fate."

"And you think I deserve mine," she said, smiling sadly. "I wonder how many others were delivered justice unfairly."

"You stole money, Amara. You're not innocent." The words were said with purpose. I wanted to be cruel, to provoke her into telling me the truth. Because she was absolutely right. I'd misjudged her, as I likely did others in the past.

However, unlike them, she had an opportunity to change fate. To provide me with a new path and a new set of targets. All I needed were the names, and I'd handle the rest.

"You know nothing about my circumstances, Killian." A fire lit her blue-green eyes, pleasing me far more than I'd allow her to see.

Yes, kitten.

Come play with me.

Tell me a story.

Tell me who to kill.

"I know the facts. You stood a man up at the altar and ran off with half his bank account." I lifted my hand to halt her impending argument. "Yes, it might be one of several accounts, but it's still a crime. Not to mention the public damage you did by leaving him on the day of your wedding." I tsked. "Poor form, sweetheart."

The fire in her gaze grew into an inferno, her stoicism finally crumbling beneath a wave of fury.

"Poor form?" she repeated, bitterness coloring her tone. "The funds in that account were set aside to complete the payments to Geoff and Clarissa Rose. *For me.* So, in my opinion, as it was my eternal servitude being purchased, the account technically belonged to me. As for leaving Malcom on our wedding day? Isn't it the duty of the bride to be a willing participant? Not a forced one? Or do you not care about that justification when evaluating a mark?"

Her cheeks were as red as her hair, her nostrils flaring. I'd struck a nerve.

And learned a hell of a lot in the process.

"He purchased you to be his trophy wife," I surmised.

She laughed, but it lacked humor. "Oh, that's a naïve assessment." She met my gaze, her pupils dilating to black out her irises. "He acquired me to fuck his friends, Killian. To fuck whomever he told me to in whatever situation he required. Including to gather intelligence and information from those he called allies, to use the details against them. And also to solidify partnerships. He obtained a woman who could play a trophy wife for the cameras while act as his deviant between the sheets. Also, that account you saw? That was the final payment. Of four."

I whistled. "So that's why he wants you back. You're an expensive investment."

Amara didn't reply, just lifted a shoulder and released a long breath that seemed to expel all her fight. "You managed to make me talk."

"I did." And I wasn't sorry about it. The only apology I would make was for misjudging her. But that truly lay at Malcom's feet, not mine, a crime he would be paying for dearly in the near future. "What types of secrets did he make you learn for him?" Because that was the key to all of this. Not who she was or how he acquired her, but what she knew as a result.

A man like Malcom could easily deny allegations associated with human trafficking, especially if Geoff and Clarissa Rose took his side. Which they would undoubtedly do. They'd paint Amara as a culprit, victim-shame her, and put her away in an insane asylum somewhere.

Or worse, have her removed.

I'd seen that sort of shit done all my life. Sure, it'd raise a few eyebrows, but in the end, the senator would find a way to garner public's sympathy. They always did.

But Amara knew something that could destroy him. Something powerful enough that he risked pissing off the Cavalieri to cover it up.

"What do you know, Amara?" I pressed, leaning toward her. "What did he reveal to you?"

She shook her head. "It doesn't matter, Killian." Her dismissive words burned, stirring a flicker of irritation.

"It doesn't matter?" I repeated, cocking a brow. "Why would you protect him?" Because that could be the only reason she'd not want to divulge information. Unless it somehow guarded her as well.

"Who says it's him I'm protecting?" she countered, confirming my suspicion.

"He has something on you." I drew my fingers through my hair, falling back against the couch. That complicated matters. "Look, the bastard tried to kill me. So regardless of whether or not you tell me what it is he has over you, he's going to keep trying to kill me. Rather than play an expensive game of cat and mouse with him, I'd much rather take him off the board entirely. Which means I need you to tell me what you know."

She studied me. "And what makes you think you can beat him?" Not a belittling question, but one laced with curiosity.

I'd intrigued her.

That meant, if I played my cards right, she'd start talking.

But I had to prove my worth to her first.

"Give me your wrist," I said, glancing at the one with the cuff.

Her brow furrowed, but she complied, lifting her delicate arm. Pressing my palm to her smooth skin, I traced the band and found the unlocking mechanism. It unlatched upon recognizing my thumbprint, falling to the couch cushion between us. "You can leave if you want, but I wouldn't recommend it." I stood to fix myself another cup of coffee while she remained on the couch, her expression wary.

She suspected this was a test.

It was, but not one designed for her. This test fell on me to pass, and failure wasn't an option.

I fixed two mugs, deciding to offer her a few shots of much-needed caffeine. If she refused, I'd drink it.

Setting the two fresh cups on the coffee table in front of the couch, I joined her again. This time I drew my leg onto the cushion and used the armrest to support my back, facing her.

"The Tabella Della Morte has a lot of resources and valuable connections, Amara. To take on such an organization means that either Malcom Jenkins is a very stupid man or he has reasons to feel confident in his position. I'm betting on the latter because your former fiancé does not strike me as an idiot. Even if he did send a bunch of amateurs to take me out."

She said nothing, her gaze unreadable as she watched me from beneath a cluster of auburn lashes. However, her lack of an argument or statement corroborated my opinion.

"Do you know how much Bedivere Corp. is worth?" I wondered, picking up my mug to blow across the rim.

"Money isn't everything," she replied.

"Whoever told you that is lying. Money is power, sweetheart." I learned that lesson a long, long time ago. "It's all about status, names, the ability to buy each other out. It's a giant fucking pissing match where the one with the most assets sits on top. Your senator is wealthy, but he's not in my league."

"Then how did Arthur blackmail you into working for him?" she asked, raising a brow. "If money is power, then you should have been able to tell him to go fuck himself."

I smiled. "Arthur Calthorpe is one of the wealthiest men in the world. He just doesn't flaunt it. That's how you run a lethal corporation like the Tabella Della Morte without government or political involvement. We kill people, Amara. Quietly. Quickly. Efficiently. But it's money that helps us thrive."

"So he's more powerful than you are," she surmised.

"Yes. Absolutely. But it's also about mutual respect." Something that had grown between us over the years. Sure, this all started because he subtly threatened to release a few images of me at a crime scene. But I didn't accept that next case out of fear. No, I accepted it out of intrigue. "He offered me the opportunity I didn't know I needed. I've never looked back."

"You enjoy killing people."

I sipped my coffee while considering how to reply to that. Being an assassin required more than a killing drive to succeed. It took concentration, discipline, and a lot of detective work. "Honestly, I enjoy the hunt more than the actual kill. But I'm skilled at both."

"You didn't bat an eye when you took down Boris and all his men." She didn't sound afraid when she recounted the actions, just matter-of-fact.

"That doesn't mean I enjoyed it."

She gave me a doubtful look. "But didn't you?"

"Did they not deserve their deaths?" I countered, curious as to how *she* felt about what happened.

"They definitely did." She didn't hesitate. "And I'm glad you killed them."

Good. "Do you think that makes you a bad person?" I wondered out loud.

"Aren't we all bad people in some way?" She leaned over to pick up the coffee mug I'd left for her and took a sip without testing the heat. Her lack of a grimace suggested a reasonable pain tolerance. "You kill for a living. I seduced for mine. And I took lives because I had no other choice.

Does that make me evil? Or willing to do anything to survive?"

"It makes you strong," I said, meaning it. "You've been through hell and lived to tell the tale."

"At least until Malcom finds me again." She stared into her coffee cup, her cheeks hollowing as she considered her next words.

I waited, not wanting to push her, not when I knew how close she was to breaking down and telling me what I needed to know.

Malcom Jenkins might be a powerful man, but he stood no chance here. I didn't care who his allies were. I'd kill them all, one by one, leaving Malcom alone and without resources. Then I'd let him sweat it out for a few days, constantly looking over his shoulder, knowing I stood somewhere nearby, ready to end him.

And only when I felt he'd suffered enough from the paranoia would I introduce him to my blade. Slowly. Purposefully. Thoroughly.

Because no one threatened my life and got away with it.

Not even the predicted future president of the United States.

AMARA

I couldn't believe I was actually considering this, but Killian addressed some impressive points. If I'd determined one thing about him by now, it was that he didn't lie. Oh, he might evade. But the man prided himself on being honest.

And his actions thus far had proven his words.

In all my years roaming the high-society circuit, I'd never heard of the Tabella Della Morte. Nor was I familiar with Arthur Calthorpe. But I supposed that was precisely the point. They remained anonymous for a reason, being called upon for the most secretive of ploys.

Such as tracking down an errant runaway slave-bride. Malcom couldn't go to the authorities without explaining his ownership of me. And he couldn't just hire any random criminal organization to find me.

No, he went to the best of the best.

To Killian.

Now, Malcom's ally had become an adversary. And the enemy of my enemy had the potential to be my new best friend.

I took another fortifying sip of the dark liquid, thankful that Killian hadn't added any cream or sugar to ruin the strong taste. He'd operated like a machine in battle tonight, taking out all of Boris's goons without flinching. While he didn't admit to enjoying it, I caught the whiff of his adrenaline in the car, noted the way it gave him life.

This man meant business.

"I'm married to my job first and foremost. And I never fail a mission." Those were his words back at the club. I'd taunted him about there being a first time for everything, yet he proved me wrong.

He was a formidable adversary.

But no longer mine.

He wanted to be allies.

"What will you do if I tell you about Malcom?" I wondered out loud.

"To you? Or to him?" he asked.

"I'm not worried about me." If Killian wanted to take down my former betrothed, then he needed me alive. "I want to know what you plan to do to Malcom."

"Dismantle his little kingdom and smoke him out. Then kill him." He tilted his head. "That includes removing the Roses, as I imagine they're tied to him in some way."

"You want to destroy all his allies."

"Yes."

"Why?"

"Because he made the mistake of trying to kill a Cavalieri. That's not something I can allow to go unpunished. And I'm certain Arthur will feel the same way."

"So you all will go after them?" How many did he say there were? Twelve? If they all were as skilled and trained as Killian, they might actually stand a chance.

"No. I'm taking this on. If I need help, I'll call them."

I choked on the coffee I'd just inhaled as a result of his proclamation. He watched while I sputtered, coughing the liquid up from my lungs, and caught my mug before I could spill any of the hot drink onto my lap.

Right.

He clearly had no idea how deep and far Malcom had rooted himself into this world if he thought he could take him out on his own.

Amir alone would require an army.

"That's impossible," I breathed.

He set both of our mugs down, then gave me his full attention. "I'll be the judge of that after you tell me what you know."

I almost laughed, my head shaking from side to side. "You have no idea what you're asking of me."

"Whatever he has against you, we can work through."

Ah, that again. He had assumed the reason I didn't want to talk was to protect Malcom. Then he jumped to this ridiculous notion that my ex-fiancé had something against me. "It's not like that. I'm not worried about me." At least not in the way he thought.

His brow furrowed. "Then what are you worried about?"

You, I almost said. Then frowned. *Why am I keeping this to myself?*

For months, I'd sworn myself to secrecy, too afraid to breathe a word of my knowledge to anyone. Not for Malcom's sake, but for my own. Yet here I sat in a hotel suite with an assassin dispatched to retrieve me or kill me. This was precisely the situation I wanted to avoid. Apart from the scenario where he actually helped me.

Such a convoluted mess.

I'd never predicted this, never even considered this an

option. My entire existence was based on my own will to survive. No one helped me. Ever.

Until Killian.

Technically, he took out those men to save himself. But he'd saved me in the process. And now he wanted revenge on Malcom.

"You want to kill him."

"Already answered that," he replied. "But if you need it repeated, yes, I am going to kill him. As well as anyone who gets in my way. And as I've already said, he's not going to stop coming after me. So you might as well tell me what it is he thinks I know."

I grimaced, that proclamation weighing heavily on my heart all over again. Because he was right. Malcom would consider him a liability just for having spent time with me.

Which meant Amir would, too.

Even if I went back to Malcom now and swore on my life that I'd not said a word, he'd still go after Killian to wrap up the loose end. He couldn't afford for anyone outside his circle to know the truth, or even suspect him of it.

"You know, as a little girl, I thought I was lucky," I said, thinking out loud. "My birth parents weren't all that well off, so when they sold me to the Rose family, I thought they wanted me to have a better life. But it was always about the money. Originally, they intended to put me in the auction right away." I gave Killian a look. "There's a market for little girls."

His expression gave nothing away, his dark eyes holding mine without a flicker of emotion.

"Well, apparently, I passed an aptitude test that set me apart from the others. And so they put me on a different track. They gave me a room upstairs filled with everything a seven-year-old could dream of, homeschooled me, and even gave me bodyguards, telling me a princess needs protection." I picked at my jeans, bitterness pooling in my mouth. "I was sixteen when I realized the truth."

Until that point, I'd bought into the lie. I thought they cared. I had so many tutors. I had friends in the house, at least until they left to join other families. I generally enjoyed my life.

But it was all a charade.

And those friends? They didn't get adopted the way I had thought.

Everything of my youth was turned on its head in a single night.

"Clarissa and Geoff had this party, and they asked me to attend. I was so excited because they usually didn't allow me to go, but they said I was finally of age." I bit the inside of my cheek. Now that turn of phrase made me sick to my stomach. "Long story short, they passed me around to the men in attendance. Let them have a proper look, as they called it. And the bidding began."

I really needed a drink.

But the look on Killian's face held me in place.

"Sixteen?" he repeated, the word sounding like a curse on his tongue. "Tell me they didn't..."

"Fuck me?" I supplied, snorting. "No. Not quite. I had to remain intact for the winning bidder, but Clarissa pledged to provide me with a healthy regimen of sexual studies in addition to my academic pursuits. The product, as she called me, was the perfect high-society bride who understood her place in the bedroom."

"And Malcom claimed the highest bid."

I smiled and shook my head. "No. Amir Assad did."

It wasn't something I knew, as I hadn't been privy to the bidding. I was just the item on the proverbial pedestal.

From the shock on Killian's expression, he definitely recognized the name. "*Amir Assad?*"

I gave him a sad grin, as if to say, *I told you that you didn't want to know.* But I kept the remark to myself and instead replied, "Yes. I was a gift. To solidify their partnership."

Which was why I knew all about their working agreement.

About the weapons Malcom was funding under the table.

About the political promises he'd made.

About the murders Amir had committed to help Malcom gain power.

Despite my short nine-month engagement to the monster, I knew everything. Not just through observation, but through my own research.

"Why didn't you run when you were in college?" he asked, flabbergasted. "My notes showed you lived on campus. Although, I couldn't find many friends outside your roommates."

"Who all happened to be bodyguards," I added. "You don't think I tried to escape? Because I did once. Learned that lesson really fast. Only my virginity had to remain intact, Killian. Everything else..." I left the sentence unfinished. He could infer the rest.

However, ironically, the biggest mistake the Roses made was providing me with a thorough education. Not only did it grant me access to computers and electronics, but it also helped me form an opinion on life.

I spent so many years assuming this was my destiny, accepting it because I saw no other way out. Then I moved in with Malcom during our engagement period and put my knowledge to the test.

Learning.

Observing.

Plotting.

"The wedding day was the only time your security team took a real break," Killian said, clearly having figured out my intentions. "And the account was the final payment. He gave you the details to give to Clarissa, didn't he?"

I nodded. "He did." Amir had transferred the funds to the account through some back-end channels, and Malcom gave me the details for Clarissa, to complete the transaction. But I took the highest amount allowed by the bank, and ran.

Killian's lips curled, not necessarily in amusement but with something that seemed akin to awe. "You had it all planned."

"And you ruined it by tracking me down." Not that I really blamed him for it. He was just doing a job.

"Well, as I said, you weren't easy to find."

"I won't apologize for that."

"Just as I won't apologize for finding you," he replied. "In fact, I'd say it's fate. Because now you've given me a list of people to track down and punish. Although, I'm going to need you to tell me everything you know about Amir Assad first."

My brow furrowed. "Hold on. You're going to kill them all?"

"That's what I said, right?"

"Just like that?"

"Just like that," he repeated. "You haven't given me anyone outside my scope. However, I have a feeling we've just skimmed the surface of what you know."

That was not what I meant. "What about me?" He couldn't possibly be planning to do all this on his own. I deserved some revenge, too.

"Worried I might kill you, kitten?" he asked, his gaze dancing over me. "Because I gotta say, I think that'd be a waste of talent."

"Damn right it would be. Which is why you'll take me

with you when you hunt these assholes down."

His amusement died. "Absolutely fucking not."

"Excuse me?"

"I work alone."

"You need me."

"Yes, for information. Not as a partner."

Oh, hell no. "So, what, they try to kill you once and suddenly your need for revenge supersedes mine?"

"That's not—"

"I wasn't done." I placed my hand on his chest and pushed him back into the couch when he tried to move, my legs straddling his thighs. "You *need* me. This is my world, Killian. I've studied it for years. I know all the players. We either do this together or not at all."

He grabbed my hips. "No, Amara."

I fisted his shirt. "I'm not asking, Killian. You want to know about Amir and Malcom? Then we work together to take them all down. Including Clarissa and Geoff." If anyone had earned a right to deliver their end, it was me. Not Killian.

"How the hell did this turn into a negotiation? I don't play with others, darling. I hunt and kill alone. Always have, always will."

I narrowed my gaze. "Then this will be the first mission you really fail, more than you already have."

"And what the fuck does that mean?"

"You almost handed me back to a monster because you believed his bullshit story. What other lies will you fall for, Killian? Because that one almost cost you your life."

He reared back as if I'd slapped him. "Did you miss the part where I killed all of them without so much as a scratch?"

"You wouldn't have even shown up at that damn meeting had you just listened to me. But your head was too far up your own ass to see reason. Just as it is now."

He glowered up at me. "The answer is still no."

"Then consider us at a standstill." I released his shirt, but his grip on my hips held me in place, our chests heaving against one another. I couldn't say why I'd put myself here. It'd just been a natural progression, my desire to be on top and in his face overruling reason.

Anger pulsed off of him, rivaling my own.

His mouth far too close to mine.

"I'm trying to help you, Amara."

"No. You're trying to help yourself. If you had my best interests in mind, then you wouldn't be trying to push me aside. You would realize and respect that I've earned this fight. I never had a choice in this life. I'm making one now, yet just like everyone else, you're trying to dictate my path for me. Which makes you no better than them."

Harsh, but true.

He had no right to tell me what I could or couldn't do. Not now. Not ever. I spent too many years battling my fate to be shoved into yet another corner.

Never again.

"I earned this," I repeated, angry tears welling in my eyes. "They tried to destroy me. They put me through hell. And you don't even know the things Malcom has made me do for him over the last nine months. He sent a couple men after you? That's so sad. He's forced me to do sadistic, twisted, fucked-up things to him, to his associates, to men I hardly knew. I've *killed* for him. Twice. Because he made me. Yet, I didn't do a thorough enough job of it. So you know what he did next? He shared me at a meeting. He made me suck—"

Killian's mouth covered mine, one of his palms sliding around the back of my neck to hold me to him when I tried to push away. Tears were streaming down my cheeks, my body trembling on top of his, and he was *kissing* me.

Not out of passion. No. This wasn't like the other times. This held a note of emotion. A heartache he couldn't seem to express with words.

My shoulders fell. My heart skipped a beat. And I melted.

All my fight gone.

Like a fire blown out in the wind.

No more arguing.

No more pain.

Just Killian.

His soft, plump lips moved against mine, releasing a compassion that mesmerized me. It stole my breath and applied a salve to my open wounds that cooled the residual burns left over from the last decade.

I wrapped my arms around his neck, holding on, needing him in a way I'd never needed anyone. He returned the embrace, his forearm a brand around my lower back, his palm searing my nape.

This was so wrong.

I shouldn't be seeking comfort from him.

But I couldn't stop, his strength the antidote to my torment.

"Killian," I whispered, uncertain of what I wanted to

say or do.

"Yes, Amara." He kissed me again, his lips worshiping mine in a way no one ever had. "Yes."

I didn't know what he meant or why he repeated the affirmation.

Or why he said it yet again.

Until suddenly I did, the reason slamming me in the chest and forcing my mouth away from his.

He gazed up at me, his irises a near black, the ire dilating his pupils a palpable presence between us. "I have two conditions."

I didn't move, our lips only a hairsbreadth apart. "Name them."

"You will follow my lead without question. It might be your home turf, but it's still my playground."

His experience made accepting that requirement easy. "And the second?" I asked.

"If things go south and you get hurt or caught, it's not on me to save you. I'm an assassin, not a knight in shining armor. So don't ever mistake me for the hero. It will get you killed. Got it?"

I swallowed, nodding. "Yes."

"Then we have a deal." He brushed his lips against

mine. "Now, I vote we continue this shit in the morning because I need some fucking sleep."

KILLIAN

Amir Assad.

A wealthy Turkish businessman known for laundering money and gun trafficking. He'd been on Arthur's watch list for years, several people ordering hits on the bastard without providing the right financial incentive.

Taking him out would not be easy, especially as he notoriously hid behind several shell corporations all over the world.

Finding him was the hard task.

But I had an idea of where to start.

"What about the girl?" Arthur asked, his voice flat over the phone. I'd just finished telling him about my conversation with Amara last night. Specifically, my freshly created kill list.

"She's too useful to discard." I didn't bother elaborating on how I'd agreed to allow her to help me. That was my

problem to handle and completely irrelevant to Arthur.

"You're fucking her."

I smirked. "Not yet." While we'd shared a bed last night, I'd slept fully clothed and armed. Trust was for the weak. I preferred to stay alive.

Although, it'd proven futile. When I awoke this morning, it was to find Amara curled into a tiny ball, passed out and oblivious.

I half expected her to try to run, had even put a few traps in place in anticipation, but she slept like a baby.

Maybe there was hope for our partnership yet.

"Well, I still think Assad could go for a higher amount, but I'll pull the highest bid. Make it hurt, Dagger."

"Without question," I replied.

"I want to review the Rose case before I sign off on that, but the senator is all yours. No one attacks my men and gets away with it."

"I'll be sure to deliver that message loud and clear." *After I demolish everything he's built.*

"Good. Keep me apprised." He hung up before I could agree. Not that he needed the words. He knew I'd call him if anything changed.

A series of documents appeared on my new tablet—

something that arrived thirty minutes after I requested it—all of which detailed Assad's last known movements.

Cairo.

Hmm. Not my favorite city. I much preferred Alexandria or Sharm el-Sheikh.

I studied the surveillance photo, noting the government agency print in the lower corner. Thank fuck for shitty security.

Assad's number one, Raoul, was last seen meeting a handful of arms dealers in downtown Cairo, which implied a pending trade. The esteemed leader would be nearby, his penchant for micromanaging notorious.

The subtle shift in the air alerted me to Amara's presence a second before she stepped through the threshold wearing last night's clothes. She appeared deliciously rumpled, her red hair a mess, her eyes warm with sleep, her cheeks a pretty flush.

If only she were naked.

Alas, we'd have to work up to that.

She possessed a sexual confidence I admired, but her background colored it in shades of black. I needed to tread carefully with this one. Even if all I wanted to do was carry her off into the bedroom and fuck her into oblivion.

"Good morning, kitten." I glanced at the clock. "Or rather, afternoon. Care for some coffee?"

"What is all this shit?" she asked, scanning the abundance of bags in the living area.

"I ordered a few things while you were catnapping." *Clothes. My tablet. A few other essential items for traveling. Some knives.* "Your bag is on the chair."

I'd noted her pant size after removing her jeans yesterday and guessed on everything else. Whatever didn't fit, she could discard.

"The carry-on you'll need for Egypt is there." I pointed to the small black suitcase on the floor. "Pack whatever you can in that. We're not checking luggage. And I'll preorder some things for arrival."

"Egypt?" she repeated.

"Mm-hmm," I murmured, pulling up a photo on the tablet. "Do you recognize him?" I showed her an image of Raoul and waited.

Her brow furrowed. "No. Who is he?"

"Assad's number one minion," I replied, sifting through more details.

"No, Taviv is his associate he uses for everything."

I blinked up at her. "Taviv?" That name didn't ring a

bell.

"Yeah." She visibly shivered, her eyes clouding over in some dark memory. "That's who he takes with him everywhere."

"You've met him."

"Yes." She swallowed and sat beside me on the couch, her thigh touching mine as she focused on my tablet. "What is this? Wait... Is that...?" She caught the emblem in the top right, causing me to smirk.

"I have backdoor access into intelligence agencies throughout the globe. Makes my job easier." Arthur had contacts in high places. So did I.

"And they don't know?"

"Pretty sure they'd be knocking down the door right now if they did." Well, and Raven would send a cryptic text of warning if anyone accessed her program. She was one of the best hackers in the world, if not *the* best. And also one of the few people who knew my true profession. Considering she worked for a notorious crime syndicate in New York City, she didn't judge. Just helped me out when needed, and I returned the favor in kind.

"How?" Amara asked, her fingers enlarging Raoul's face.

"I was hired for a job in New York City once. The mark was swindling money from his superiors, and also an asshole who liked to take advantage of his employees. One of those employees was a woman with a knack for computers. She granted me access to her systems as a thank-you." I shrugged. "You'd like her."

"Is she one of your girlfriends?" Amara wondered, her tone deceptively casual. She busied herself by flipping to another screen on my tablet—the profile on Assad.

"I don't have any girlfriends," I replied, watching her. "And Raven is just a friend. I wouldn't jeopardize that by fucking her." I wasn't a saint, but I also didn't sleep around much. Just the occasional fling whenever the opportunity was right.

Amara nodded, tugging her lip between her teeth as she started scrolling through images on my tablet with her finger. She shifted to tuck her legs beneath her, angling her body toward mine. I stretched my arm out across the top of the couch behind her while holding the device for her in my opposite hand.

"What's wrong with your tattoos?" I asked, noting the discoloration along her left arm.

"Hmm?" She glanced at her shoulder. "Oh. Yeah. I

guess they're fading now. Too bad. I kind of liked them."

"They're fake?" I never would have guessed that, but probably should have considering all the photos I had of her from the job revealed porcelain skin with no tattoos. Of course, it'd been her face I memorized more than her body. Mmm, I would fix that soon. Very soon.

"Part of Scarlet Rosalind's persona," she replied, her brow furrowing as she enlarged another photo. "There. That's Taviv."

I eyed the back of a man's head. "How do you know?"

"Trust me. It's him." She shivered again, whatever he'd done to her evident in the way she shuttered her expression. "He never leaves Amir's side."

"A bodyguard," I translated. Or maybe *enforcer* was the better term. "Raoul is his primary business associate."

She shook her head again. "No. When it's important, he sends Taviv."

"Raoul is noted as his negotiator." I lifted my arm, needing my opposite hand, and skimmed through all the screens to pull up the man's profile. "See."

Amara took the item from me and began reading the profile, her gorgeous eyes flickering as she took in all the details. Her lips pinched to the side. "No. He might use this guy for his less important deals, but he's not important to Amir. Those he trusts most, he meets in person and keeps near him."

"Like Jenkins?" I asked.

"That's complicated." She set the tablet in my lap, her attention on me. "I was a gift from Amir to Malcom, a way to finalize their partnership. No one outside a few people know, which is why Taviv is usually the one who meets with Malcom."

"And that's why you're saying he's Assad's true right-hand man, because otherwise it would be Raoul."

"Yes. I've never seen Raoul before, and the things Amir has planned, he would want his lieutenants involved."

"What do they have planned?" I asked, setting the tablet to the side and giving her my full attention.

"To ensure Malcom becomes the next president of the United States. To give him the power and ability to remain in charge due to a cataclysmic series of events that will require an extension of his presidency. To solidify his alliances with certain countries. There's a whole plan that's already in motion, and Malcom thinks he's in charge. But it's really Amir. He's the true mastermind."

That sounded about on par with what I knew of the

crime lord. He had a myriad of contacts throughout the world, all partnerships created through years of weapons trading and other items. Like biological and chemical warfare. He had access to it all and profited significantly from war—hence his operations in the Middle East, a known hub for conflict.

"I need a list." I stood, searching for a pad of paper and a pen, and handed them to her on the couch. "List every name you can think of, including Malcom's political partners—both good and bad. Put a positive sign next to anyone you consider to be decent and not involved. A negative sign beside those with known ties to his nefarious activities. And a check mark beside those we should kill. You work on that while I make you some fresh coffee."

I didn't offer to add anything to it since she seemed okay without the sugar and cream last night.

"Okay." She bent her head, already writing.

Having her agreeable and compliant was new. I rather liked it. "I'll order us some food, too." Because I was starving.

She just nodded, her focus on the task.

An hour later, our lunch finally arrived and Amara handed me three pages of names. I noted several senators and other politicians on the list, most of which she marked with positive signs. One had an X beside it—Senator Dresden.

"Did you ever meet Senator Dresden?" I asked, very aware of the name and the senator's darker inclinations.

"Yes. At a charity event. He's dead now. That's why I added the X." She took a bite of her spätzle dish. There were mushrooms in it, but no meat.

"I know." From what Nikolai told me, Senator Dresden had more than deserved his fate. "What about the other two Xs?" I knew she meant they were dead, but didn't know much about them.

"Sharsky was a governor that Malcom made me suck off and kill after gathering some information. Wilson was a political analyst for one of Malcom's political rivals. He gave me to Wilson for a night in exchange for some answers, then had me poison him after we were done."

The casual way she recounted the horrors of her past made my stomach churn. No one should have endured what she went through. However, that she did so and maintained her sanity spoke volumes about her character. Every time she spoke, my admiration for her went up another notch.

"This is good," she said, pointing to her food. "You should try it."

I smirked. "Nah, the currywurst is the best." And something that hadn't been on the hotel menu. It required a special delivery, which Wyatt's brother really needed to address. Currywurst was a fucking staple in this country. To not have it on the hotel menu was criminal.

We ate in silence while I reviewed the names. So many allies, the majority of which had positive signs because they were political connections. About fifteen others had negative marks, only two of which were senators, the others being wealthy patrons.

And then only a handful were marked for death. "Why are there only seven check marks on this list, Amara?" I expected at least twenty. Yet she'd only checked Assad, Taviv, Malcom, and four notable campaign donors.

"You asked me to check the ones I want dead. Those are the seven."

"And none of these other men did something that warrants a death sentence?" Because I recognized several who I knew did. "You're telling me none of these other guys touched you? Or asked Malcom for a night with you?"

She set her mostly finished dish down and faced me on the couch. "Some of them are horny men, yes. But Malcom is the one who offered me to them."

"And they *accepted*. They had to know it was wrong."

"So you want me to kill them for touching me against my will?"

"No, *I* want to kill them for touching you without consent."

"By that logic, then I should add you to the list. I mean, you put a knife against my pussy just yesterday, didn't you? And I don't recall asking for that."

My jaw dropped at the crude words, my lunch churning in my gut. I pushed the plate aside, my appetite diminished.

"What? So you're allowed to take advantage of me, but none of the others can?" She tsked. "Come on now, Killian. You have to admit that's a bit of the pot calling the kettle black, isn't it?" Such flippant words spoken in a chastising manner that grated on my nerves.

"So you liked them touching you?" I countered, irked that she'd just compared me to a bunch of rapists. Yes, I may have taken advantage of a compromising situation, but only because the attraction between us was thriving and mutual.

"Sometimes the body responds even when your mind rebels," she replied, glancing downward in shame.

I caught her chin and forced her to meet my gaze. "Are you trying to tell me you didn't like my knife against you? That your body responded against your will?" Because I wouldn't believe her for a second. I knew how to read women. Her interest had darkened her gaze to a luscious green, and she'd certainly kissed me back. Fuck bodily reactions. She'd *liked* my touch.

"No." She tried to shake off my hand, but I held her captive, needing to know the answer to this, to read the truth of it in her eyes. "You asked if I liked them touching me. I'm saying that not all bodily reactions are willing. So while I may have *reacted* for them, it doesn't mean I enjoyed it."

"And with me?" I pressed.

She swallowed, her pupils dilating. "You're... different."

Good. "Then don't you ever put me in the same category as *them*. I may like playing with you, Amara, but I would never accept the bride of another man for a night when I knew it was against her will." I released her, still furious that she would even think to compare us.

But of course she would.

That was all she'd ever known.

"Take this list and put an asterisk by the ones who touched you." Since it seemed she'd never been with a man willingly, it wasn't worth having to clarify any specific parameters. I handed her the papers without looking at her, too irritated with myself and her to trust my expression.

"A lot of them expressed interest in scheduling time with me for after the wedding," she said quietly instead of doing what I asked. "I was only with Malcom at his residence for nine months, and most of the men who touched me in that time were members of his staff, like Boris." Her wince shook the couch, stirring a pit of unease inside me.

This woman had gone through hell and came out on the other side fighting. And here I was angry that she'd accused me of being a monster like Malcom when she had every right to believe that. Amara and I met because I was sent to drag her home—alive or dead. That made me a villain in her eyes, one who had touched her just like all the others.

Different, she'd called me. Different because she was actually attracted to me? Or different because I was helping her?

"I mean, there was the first night when he took my virginity and then passed me around to a bunch of his colleagues to see how much I could endure before breaking. Then he used me a few times at meetings, mostly as an ornament for the table. Except for one time when I upset him. He made me perform then. Oh, and the two times he sent me out to act as a black widow. But the majority of his plans for me were post-wedding. Everything during our engagement was merely a test of my usefulness, both for him and for Amir."

My blood boiled at how casually she depicted the last few months of her life. Could it have been worse? Absolutely. But *fuck*, what that bastard did to her was so damn wrong. And his intentions for the future?

"I'm going to enjoy destroying him," I admitted, my tone darkened by lethal intent. "I still want to know who on this list touched you. Even if it was just a stroke of a finger across your skin, I want his fucking name identified. We might not kill each one, but we will be sending them all a message." And they'd go on a watch list. If they so much as breathed wrong, I'd have their balls in a vise. "Also, add Clarissa and Geoff, and anyone else involved in the auctions."

"You're going to have me writing all day," she grumbled.

"Thorough planning is required, kitten. Especially for what we intend to accomplish." I stood, needing a shower after this discussion. She wasn't the first to lay hefty allegations at my feet, but she was the first to work her way beneath my skin. Because while I knew her accusations were born from a fucked-up history, she was partly right. I'd never asked for permission. It just wasn't my style. I relied on my partners to tell me if I pushed too far, and I enjoyed the danger of knife play. I thought Amara had, too.

Now I didn't know what to think.

And I hated that.

I brushed my fingers through my hair, frozen before her. "Amara?"

She didn't look at me, her focus on the papers in her lap. "Hmm?"

I caught her chin again, lifting her gaze to mine. "If I ever do something to you that you don't like, you will tell me."

"Like tagging me with a bracelet that can explode?" she asked, cocking a brow.

A snort tickled my throat. "I did that for the mission."

"Yes, I know." She covered my hand with her own, her fingers delicate over mine. "You've not done anything to hurt me. I'm fine."

"I fired a gun at you."

"And I shot you full of ketamine." She shrugged. "I'm not fragile, Killian. I don't break easily." She actually sounded offended that I might think otherwise, which brought me to my knees before her.

"I don't think you're weak at all, Amara. What I'm saying is, if I try to push you too far, I need you to tell me. Because I'm not used to asking. I take. Consent is usually implied. But your situation makes that, well, different." I used the word intentionally, something she noted, because her nostrils flared and her gaze narrowed.

"I meant that I'm attracted to you, jackass. Stop overthinking it, or you'll ruin our dynamic and I won't be attracted to you anymore."

My eyebrows lifted. "Is that a threat?"

"Yes. It is." The look she gave me set my blood on fire—all challenge and heat and sexy as fuck. This woman allured me in a way no one else ever had.

A warrior.

An equal.

My kind of lover.

"Threat acknowledged and accepted." I brushed my nose against hers, our mouths a hairsbreadth apart. "Now, while you work, I'm going to take a shower and daydream about how hot your pretty little cunt will feel around my cock when I eventually fuck you. Because, darling Amara, it's going to happen. And soon. But I need that list from you first."

Her mouth parted beneath mine, giving me the opportunity I craved. My tongue slid inside with ease, possessing her in the way I intended to possess her body, demonstrating my intentions with each thrust and stroke until I left her panting against me.

"Mmm, and you're going to enjoy it, too," I whispered, the words a promise and a vow. "Have fun working, kitten."

AMARA

This is not going to end well. Killian seemed to feel otherwise as he entered the international customs area, his suit jacket concealing the knives I knew he carried beneath. He shook hands with one of the agents, handing him paperwork of some kind, then gestured to me and said something in fluent Arabic.

How many languages does this man know? I filed the question away for later, nervous as hell inside Cario's airport.

"*Shukraan,*" Killian said, bowing slightly to the heavyset male holding our fake passports. The border agent replied with a few words I didn't understand, sending us on our way.

Killian nodded, accepting the passports and his document while saying "*Shukraan*" again. He tucked the items into his briefcase, then held out his hand for mine. I

accepted, following his lead.

We'd spent a week in that hotel room together, where we went over every minute detail of my life with Malcom, reviewed several plans, and monitored our targets from his tablet. The woman who had hooked Killian up with the backdoor access to all the government surveillance systems deserved a medal.

Because damn, was it helpful. And it put me at ease being able to pull up Malcom's whereabouts with a few clicks. Killian had showed me that little detail our second day together in the hotel, his way of assuring me that my former fiancé was nowhere near us. I'd worried he might find me with us being so close to the original pickup point, but Killian said that was all part of his plan. Malcom would expect us to run. And so we didn't.

Killian led us down a hallway separate from the other customs lines, a guard at our back. I feigned an ease I didn't feel at his side, pretending this was all expected and not at all terrifying.

Especially as I had two daggers tucked into the black boots beneath my floor-length dress. As we'd taken a private jet from Berlin, there hadn't been any sort of security for us when boarding. And it appeared we weren't going to have any here, either.

Doors with a view of the outside loomed ahead, two more soldier types standing guard on either side. The male behind us said something that earned him a solitary nod. A warm breeze hit my face as the glass shifted, revealing a waiting car just outside.

This one was a less conspicuous black sedan. Killian accepted the keys from the man waiting for us beside the trunk and put my small bag inside, followed by his briefcase. He hadn't bothered with a carry-on apart from that. I'd crammed my bag full of stuff from my backpack and the clothing he'd procured for me in Berlin. The hotel's laundry service had been useful, even if Killian remarked about it being unnecessary. Apparently, he'd ordered another wardrobe for our stay here.

I supposed a man of his profession required these things, constantly moving around and tracking new targets.

He uttered a few words in Arabic before opening my door and gesturing for me to enter. I slid over the leather interior, folding my dress around my legs, and sighed as the air-conditioning ruffled my hair.

No incidents. We're fine. I'm fine. This is all fine.

Except I didn't feel fine.

Our purpose here was to track down Raoul and send a message to Amir. One I really didn't want to deliver but Killian assured was necessary.

He joined me in the car, his tailored suit giving him an elegant look that paired nicely with his styled hair and aristocratic features. "In retrospect, I'm glad the tattoos are gone. At least for now."

I frowned at my bare arms, exposed in my sleeveless dress. "What? Why?" I sort of missed the color.

"Because you'd stand out considerably in Cairo with ink on your skin, and we need to blend in, not call attention to ourselves." He pulled on his seat belt, finished fussing over the controls, and shifted the car into gear. "You can breathe now, Amara." He sounded amused.

"I'm breathing just fine."

"Uh-huh." His lips curled. "I thought you were going to pass out at customs."

"Did you see all the machine guns?" I countered.

He snorted. "The majority of those guys are amateurs. They wouldn't be able to hit a moving target."

"Machine guns just require you to pull the trigger. Not much skill needed."

"Sure, when up against an average person." He pulled

away from the terminal, his ease with navigating our surroundings confirming his familiarity with Cairo. "I'm not average, Amara."

"I am."

"No, darling. You certainly are not." He reached over to grab my hand and brought it to his lips. But rather than kiss my skin, he nipped my racing pulse and chuckled when I jumped. "This is going to be fun."

"No, it's not. Amir isn't someone we should be taunting."

"Ah, but I want him to come out and play." He placed my palm against his thigh, his hand returning to the shifter as he exited the airport. "A man like Assad needs to be inspired to venture outside of his safe haven. We're here to inspire him."

By assassinating Raoul.

Killian had an entire itinerary of activities lined up for us, all revolving around the other man's perceived schedule. He wanted to identify the perfect time and location to take the man down. Then we'd move on to phase two.

I studied the scenery as we drove, noting the insanity of the highway system, the surrounding buildings with open balconies and busy roofs, and the yellowish sky beyond.

"Do you think we'll see the pyramids while we're here?" I wondered out loud, disappointed that we hadn't seen them from the plane. Killian told me they were right next to the city, but the haze as we landed made it impossible to see.

"If you want," he replied, his thigh tensing beneath my palm as he downshifted in the early evening traffic. "We can make it a celebratory trip after we handle Raoul."

"I'd like that," I admitted. He already knew this was my first time to Egypt, that while I'd visited Europe several times, I'd never ventured south to the Middle East. Over the last week, I learned there were not many places Killian hadn't seen, his profession and background sending him all over the world, all the time.

Despite the flirtatious behavior and seductive words, he'd not done much more than kiss me. He was clearly taking it slow because of my previous experiences, or maybe he wanted me to make a move. But whenever I considered it, a new plan came up and we ended up talking it through until I could barely keep my eyes open.

Killian was definitely thorough.

And brilliant.

And sexy as sin in that suit.

I glanced away, but not before I caught the upward twitch of his mouth. He always seemed to know when I was looking at him. Which, I supposed, made sense, what with him being a skilled assassin and all.

"How do you know so many languages?" I asked, thoughts of his lethal talents reminding me of his proficient cover story at the airport.

"School. Life. Experience." He shrugged. "I studied Latin as an adolescent, which made learning Spanish, Portuguese, and Italian easy. I'm not very proficient in French, but I understand it. German was something I studied in high school. Arabic is a language I took in college, as well as Farsi. I'd like to learn Urdu someday."

"What? No interest in Russian?" I joked.

"Nah, if the case requires Russian, I just call Nikolai."

"Nikolai?" I repeated.

"One of my best friends." His lips curled. "Another Cavalieri. He's the only one helping with some of the items on our list."

I frowned. "Which ones?"

"The two campaign donors who have homes in Florida—Davidson and Kirpatrick."

My blood ran cold at the mention of two of Malcom's

best friends. They'd been there my first night. The one where… where I became acquainted with Malcom for the first time.

It was Kirpatrick who had finally broken me.

Bile rose in my throat at the thought, my body turning to ice.

Killian laid his too-hot palm over mine and brought my hand up to his mouth for a kiss. "They'll never touch you again, Amara," he murmured. "And trust me, Nikolai and Ava will be sure to make it hurt."

I swallowed, my heart thundering in my ears. Not just from the memory, but also from the realization that we were doing this. That Killian was really helping me.

No one had helped me before.

Everyone just used me.

I didn't know how to accept this, how to process the feelings behind it. It wasn't completely for me, but a form of revenge for Killian, too. He wanted to destroy Malcom for trying to kill him. I understood that.

Yet, somehow, this had become deeper.

Because Killian made me add Clarissa and Geoff, and all their known associates, to our list. And none of them bore value to his ultimate goal, because Malcom's ties to the auction circuit were minimal, me being the only link.

Which meant Killian only intended to kill them all as a way to seek justice.

For me.

And for the multitude of lives they'd ruined.

He kissed my hand again before releasing me in favor of the gearshift. "We have dinner plans at eight near Raoul's expected location. I want to take a walk around the area, survey the security and whatnot. Tomorrow, the fun starts."

"Fun," I repeated. "Right."

He chuckled. "You'll see, kitten."

I just shook my head. Him and that nickname. I wouldn't tell him that I liked it. That it turned me on every time he used it. That I dreamed of him whispering that endearment in my ear after giving me a crude command.

Suck my cock, kitten.

Ride me, kitten.

Mmm, I'm going to devour that sweet cunt, kitten. Make you scream for hours.

My thighs clenched, the need coursing through me a cruel taunt. I'd never wanted a man like I wanted Killian. And he seemed to be enjoying torturing me as a result.

Maybe I just needed to jump him.

Take off all my clothes and demand he fuck me.

I knew how to seduce a man, so why was Killian so different?

Because you like him, my mind whispered.

I growled in response, irritated. *That should make this easier, not harder.*

"You all right over there?" Killian asked, his amusement palpable. He probably knew he was driving me insane with lust. *Jackhole.*

"I'm fine."

"Are you? Because I swear you just growled at me."

"I growled at myself," I grumbled, watching the scenery change from highway to side streets.

"Mmm, well, feel free to growl at me anytime, kitten. It's hot."

I rolled my eyes. "You're all talk and no action, Bedivere. I'm not worried."

He laughed. "Excuse me?"

Shit. I hadn't meant to say that out loud. "Nothing."

"Oh, no, that was something all right." He pulled up to a stoplight and turned toward me. "Did you just accuse me of having performance issues?"

"Do you?" I countered, deciding to take his bait. "Because I thought you wanted to fuck me. And you haven't."

"Eager, kitten?" he asked softly, danger glittering in his dark eyes. "Maybe I consider all this dancing around each other to be foreplay."

"Maybe I consider it boring."

"Then you wouldn't be over there all hot and bothered and growling, would you?" He smirked and refocused on the road. "Patience, sweet Amara. You'll feel my cock soon."

"All talk and no action," I repeated, sighing. "Here I thought you knew how to handle a woman, Killian."

He chuckled. "Baiting me isn't going to work."

Yeah? We'll see about that, Bedivere.

Because I had a few ideas on how to properly *bait* him. I just needed the courage to follow through.

Killian presented a challenge unlike any I'd ever faced. He intrigued me. He turned me on. All of which were new and enticing sensations. And I wanted to see how deep it could all go, to see if he had the ability to shatter my past and help me move on from the history shackling my emotions.

I wanted him to introduce me to life. To passion. To

ecstasy.

Why I'd chosen him, I couldn't say. Maybe because he was the first to ever care. Maybe because he awoke all these foreign feelings inside me. Maybe because I trusted him, at least on a superficial level.

Or maybe all of those reasons wrapped up into one big reason—I just desired him.

He wasn't my knight.

He wasn't my savior.

He was merely Killian. *My Killian.* At least for now. And I wanted to know what that meant and how it felt to be well and truly possessed by a man of his knowledge and power.

So perhaps I needed to show him that, to convince him with my body instead of my words. Before he drew this out too long and ruined the connection between us.

Because if there was one thing I knew, it was that nothing good lasted forever.

Tonight, I decided. *Tonight, I'll play him at his own game.*

KILLIAN

"*As-salaam 'alaykum,*" the lanky host greeted as we entered the restaurant.

"*Wa 'alaykum al-salaam,*" I replied.

"Welcome to Cairo, Mister and Mrs. Dagger," he added, his eyes smiling excitedly. The kid must be studying English and eager to practice.

Amara's hand tightened around mine, as it had all evening every time someone addressed us as a wedded couple. It was the alias I'd chosen for this trip. The only people who knew me by the nickname of Dagger were the Cavalieri and Arthur. It made for an excellent code name, considering my affinity for knives.

And tonight, I was Mr. Cav Dagger, just as I'd been in Germany. But Amara was playing the role of my wife, Scarlet Dagger.

Both identities held diplomatic immunity, hence

our unique entrance at Cairo International Airport. Raven worked some magic for me to acquire the right documentation, something she did in addition to helping me with Amara's new passport. I sent her a large sum of money to show my gratitude, and she sent me back a photo of her middle finger. Apparently, she didn't appreciate the gesture.

I pulled the chair out for Amara, playing the part of gentleman. Then took my seat across from her. I'd chosen this restaurant because I suspected Raoul resided nearby and the records suggested he dined here often.

Unfortunately, I didn't see him here tonight.

But maybe we'd get lucky.

"The entire menu is in Arabic," Amara murmured, eyeing the placard on her plate.

It was a fairly straightforward menu. Not a lot of options. But the online ratings suggested it as one of the best in Cairo. "Do you prefer beef, lamb, or chicken?"

She twisted her mouth to the side. "Uh, depends on how it's cooked. Do you have a recommendation?"

"Lamb."

"Then I'll have lamb."

I smiled. "I like it when you're agreeable, Amara."

"Should I have chosen beef?"

"Definitely not." I signaled for the waiter and ordered our main dishes with a few sides. My Arabic accent wasn't perfect, mainly because the Egyptian dialect differed significantly from the formal language I studied in college. Thankfully, most television shows and movies were in Egyptian Arabic, helping me to learn various colloquialisms. Which I used now.

Amara wore an intrigued expression when we finished, her blue-green irises flaring with interest.

"What do you want to know, darling?" I asked before sipping from my glass of water on the table, then relaxed into my chair to admire the neckline of her long-sleeved dress. Modest—because we were in Egypt—but delectably enticing. And tight, too.

She bit her lip, her cheeks flushing a pretty shade of pink. "I'm just amused by your ability to fluctuate between languages."

"Says the woman who speaks German." I tilted my head, curious. "What other languages do you know, Amara?"

"I'm not fluent; I just understand it. Same with French, Spanish, and Turkish."

"Turkish?" I repeated. "That's different."

She shrugged. "My birth mother spoke it. I don't remember much, but I can pick up words here and there."

"Were you born in Turkey?" I wondered, unclear of her true origin.

"I don't know," she admitted. "My background is fuzzy. We moved around a lot. I rarely saw my father, can't even tell you what he looked like, actually." Another shrug. "I remember being in South Carolina with my mother. Then all I can recall is Boston, where the Roses raised me."

"You said the Roses move a lot as well?"

"Clarissa, yes. But I stayed with Geoff in Boston. They homeschooled me, then sent me to Harvard for my undergrad."

With bodyguards, she failed to add. Bodyguards whom I'd added to my kill list after learning more about them this week.

Our waiter appeared with a serving of tea, offering it to Amara first and then to me. She sipped the warm liquid tentatively, then drank a little more after deciding she liked the unique mint flavoring. I joined her in the silence, content to just observe her a little without words.

We did this throughout the week, lapsing into a

comfortable companionship that required no conversation. It was as if we just understood each other. Which made no sense because our backgrounds couldn't be more different. She grew up a slave, trained to serve a future husband. I grew up with loving parents and wanted for nothing.

Yet neither of us turned out as expected.

Maybe that was what brought us close together—the fact that we surpassed all expectations and chose our own routes. Me, an assassin. Her, a warrior. The perfect pairing. When she first demanded to work with me, I balked. Now, I could see why it would work. She actually followed my lead, allowing my experience to be her guide, and in turn offered unique perspectives.

Such as her insight into Assad's true network.

And while she didn't want to leave a message for Assad and Malcom, she trusted my plan.

Amazing.

"You're staring," she whispered.

"I am." Because she was one of the most beautiful women I'd ever met. Her battered soul lurked in her gaze, calling to me to soothe her, to show her that not everyone in this world was evil. It both scared me and enthralled me, making me want to accept the challenge and run from it at the same time.

But I wasn't someone who backed away from difficult tasks.

I was the guy who accepted them, and beat them.

Did that make me a hero or a competitor? Did I pursue her for selfish reasons or selfless ones? I really didn't know. Perhaps it was a mixture of both. I wanted to be the one who healed her, to introduce her to true sensuality and feeling.

I wanted to be her champion.

Which wasn't me at all. And yet, it suited me, too. Because I always won, and right now, Amara appealed to me as a prize.

But I had to be worthy of that reward. *That* was why I took this slow, breaking down her barriers one by one and demonstrating what a courtship should feel like. Even if our situation was fucked up and complicated, she deserved that much. And the smile she gave me now said it was working.

She shook her head. "I don't know what you're thinking, but it's making me want to growl again."

My lips twitched. "Good. I like that sound."

"God, Killian, why are we dancing around this?" she

demanded. "Why are you making me wait?"

"Because it'll be that much better in the end. Trust me."

"No one has ever done this to me before."

"Which is exactly why I'm doing it now," I replied.

She pouted, causing my cock to twitch. I wanted to feel those lips wrapped around me. Maybe I would tonight. "But you know I want you," she said, sounding adorably frustrated.

I glanced around to make sure no one was eavesdropping, then I leaned in, holding her gaze. "Are you wearing panties, Amara?"

Her nostrils flared, her pupils dilating. "I... yes. Why?"

"Give them to me."

"What?"

I smiled. "You heard me, kitten."

"Here?" she squeaked, her cheeks flushing a gorgeous crimson.

"Yes." I leaned in further, dropping my voice to a murmur. "You said you want me. I want proof. Right now."

The hitch in her breath was music to my ears, as was the delectable blush painting her subtle cleavage. "I..."

I cocked a brow. "Did I stutter, darling?"

"N-no."

"Then why aren't you complying? Or is it that you're not as interested as you claim?" I relaxed in my chair, allowing the taunt to settle between us.

She narrowed her gaze. "You think I won't do it?"

"I don't see you doing it," I replied, lifting my water to hide my smile against the rim. "I never took you for a coward, kitten. Pity."

Her resulting growl went straight to my groin, tightening my balls in anticipation and excitement. We had nothing else planned for the evening other than a stroll around the area to scope out Raoul's favorite hangouts. That gave me hours to indulge in her back at the hotel, a temptation I put on hold for the last week, the need to plan having been our priority.

But now we had our plan.

It'd already started.

That gave me a few minutes to breathe, to relax, to *enjoy*.

Mixing business with pleasure appeared to have its benefits, and I intended to explore those benefits thoroughly.

Amara licked her lips, her chest rising and falling in both anger and exhilaration. Mmm, I bet the lace between her thighs was soaked with her interest. I couldn't wait to taste it.

Her hands slowly disappeared beneath the table, her blue-green irises locked on mine. Heat and arousal simmered between us, a palpable, heady indulgence that heated my blood and lengthened my cock.

I wanted her.

Badly.

And I let her see it in my gaze.

She shifted in her chair, and I imagined her rolling her floor-length dress upward, exposing her sexy legs inch by slow inch. A slit gown would have made this task easier, but I didn't do easy. I preferred to work. It heightened the reward.

She bit her lower lip as she lifted just enough to hint at what she was doing. Rather than glance around, she focused on me, her confidence in the act arousing as hell.

"If you don't fuck me later, we're going to have words," she said, her voice a throaty purr.

"So demanding," I teased. "What happened to foreplay?"

"This last week has been foreplay on steroids, and you know it." She bent, causing her top to lower over her breasts and providing me with a tantalizing view of creamy skin. And then she straightened. "Enjoy." She reached across the table to drop her lacy thong on my empty plate.

"Looks delicious," I replied, my lips curling. "Shall I give it a taste, kitten?"

She swallowed, her face matching her alias—*Scarlet*.

I lifted the delicate black lace and pressed it to my nose, inhaling her addictive scent. "Mmm, these are soaked through." Noting the way she squirmed, I added, "Perhaps you do want something from me after all."

"Killian," she breathed, her nipples prominent beneath the thin fabric of her dress. "People are watching."

Yes, it did appear that the couple sitting a table over was watching us with slacked jaws. I gave in to the urge to lick the damp fabric, slowly and deliberately, while holding her heated gaze. "Dessert before dinner." I allowed myself another taste, humming in approval. "I approve, Amara."

I folded the undergarment and tucked it into my jacket pocket, eliciting gasps from the pair of gawkers observing us. I gave the woman a wink, which caused her cheeks to deepen to a blood-red color. Her husband appeared ready to have a word, something I suggested he stop considering with a quick glance.

What Amara and I did was our business. Not his. No one asked him to watch.

I reached out for her hand and brought it to my lips, placing an open-mouthed kiss on her wrist. "Thank you for the appetizer, kitten."

She shivered. "I swear, if you don't follow through..." She trailed off, shaking her head.

"Finish that threat," I dared, amused.

"I'll sleep naked. I'll pleasure myself beside you and make you watch. And when you try to touch me, I'll refuse."

"Delayed gratification is my favorite," I warned her. "And I'll use those punishments against you as well, sweetheart."

"All talk," she accused, yet again. "All talk."

I chuckled darkly. "Oh, you will wish it was all talk later." She'd met my blade, but that was merely an introduction. The Cavalieri called me *Dagger* because of my sharp skills in the field and my proclivity for using knives in the bedroom.

Amara would learn.

And she would beg for more.

Her lips parted as I allowed her a glimpse of the lethal promise beneath my skin. Sensual, yes. Deadly, too.

The urge to enlighten her with a thorough demonstration at the table hit me hard in the gut.

Then the door opened.

And Raoul entered.

I took another sip from my glass before catching Amara's smoldering stare again. She hadn't noticed our newcomer yet, too focused on me to look anywhere else.

"You know that message we discussed? I might be delivering it tonight," I said casually as four men in suits walked in, joining Raoul.

Crime lords.

All of them.

The interest in Amara's eyes died, but she didn't otherwise move. A natural at deception, something I approved of greatly. Working together was turning out to be a lot more exciting than I originally anticipated.

Maybe I could recruit her for more missions in the future. It would be a good reason to allow her to live, what with having divulged everything about the Tabella Della Morte to her. Arthur would not be amused when I revealed that fact, though he had to know already. It was the only way to make Amara talk. She required trust, not torture.

Our food arrived just as Raoul and his party were

seated on the other side of the restaurant, their table in perfect view of ours. It was as though fate had delivered me the winning hand.

The waiter returned with more water and tea, then left us to our meal. Which Amara seemed unable to touch.

I placed a few kebabs and a spoonful of rice on her plate. "Eat, or you'll draw attention to yourself," I informed her quietly while serving myself twice the amount. "I won't let him near you." I knew that was what had her nervous— she couldn't see Raoul. It didn't matter that they weren't acquainted; he worked for the man who bought her. I understood her reservations.

Amara cleared her throat, giving me a nod. "Okay." That single word warmed my heart because it signified trust. I promised to have her back and she believed me. It was a gift I gladly accepted.

She used her fork to remove the lamb and veggies from the stick, then picked up a few pieces of pita bread to create what appeared to be tacos. Or perhaps it was her version of gyros. She layered the bottom of one with hummus, added some meat and rice, and took a bite.

I swallowed my chuckle, admiring her for trying, and decided to follow suit. Because hey, it sounded good. So what if she was supposed to eat with her fork?

We dined in silence, her focus on me while I casually observed our quarry across the room. The couple dining nearby left partway through, but not without a few pointed glances our way that had my lips twitching.

"I think his wife is jealous of our kink," I murmured, winking again at the woman. She turned a shade of purple as her husband practically pushed her out of the restaurant.

Amara shook her head. "You're bad."

"I know," I agreed, taking another bite. "What do you think of your kebab taco?"

"It's good." She created another and took a bite, her gaze twinkling. At least she'd calmed down a bit, falling into our date once more. If Raoul didn't have half of my attention, I'd have leaned across the table to tease her a bit. Especially as she no longer wore panties.

Mmm. We'd play later.

In fact, with the opportunity before us, I could just get this part of the mission over with now and move us forward a step on the list.

I swirled my water, wishing it was a scotch or a bourbon. Alas, alcohol in Cairo was uncommon. Another reason to accelerate the plan.

We were only here to deliver a message. The true fun would begin back in the States.

As if hearing my thoughts, Raoul stood and walked right past our table on the way to the restrooms. *Oh, this is too easy.*

Amara's lips parted slightly upon finally seeing him. Having studied his photos all week, she easily recognized him, even from behind.

I counted ten beats before pushing out my chair. "Darling, can you excuse me for a moment?"

Her face paled. "Killian——"

I brushed my thumb over her lips, giving her a smile. "I'll just be a few minutes. Trust me." I didn't give her a chance to object, merely followed Raoul's trail toward the back of the restaurant.

One bathroom.

Locked.

It gave me a chance to scope out the security. No cameras. The door to the kitchen was locked and closed, suggesting employees rarely used this entryway. And we were out of view of the restaurant patrons.

Some might find it superstitious to be dealt such a perfect hand, but I knew better. Most circumstances in life occurred in perfect order; it was human involvement that fucked it all up.

And the only thing that could go wrong now was someone joining me in line, which provided me with the incentive to hurry this along.

I eyed the handle, noting the cheap lock. A stern twist would shatter it. And I doubt a door like this had a deadbolt.

Pressing my ear against the door, I waited for the sound of a flush, knowing it would indicate a moment of weakness.

There.

I twisted the handle hard, forcing the door open and clocking the idiot right in the head. Not part of my plan, but it worked. He growled a curse in Arabic while I kicked the door closed behind me and pushed him toward the sink.

"Didn't anyone ever teach you to wash your damn hands? Fuck, man." Finding nothing to bar the door, I grabbed him by the lapels of his jacket and shoved him against it. He was so dazed and shocked from my abruptness that he didn't go for his gun until a second too late. I already had it in my hand, the barrel lifting to his temple.

"*Marhabaan*," I greeted, giving him a too-friendly smile. "I know you speak English, asshole, so I'll get right to the point. I need you to call your boss for me." I glanced down, regretting it instantly. "And finish zipping up your fucking pants."

Seriously.

He was he going to walk into the hallway undone? Because he clearly hadn't planned to wash his hands. Poor hygiene all around.

"You have a death wish," he replied, his accent holding a slight British lilt.

"I could say the same thing about you for misinterpreting my words as a request." I dug the barrel into the side of his head. "Pants. Now."

He grumbled out a poorly chosen word as he finished buttoning up, then cocked a brow. "Satisfied?"

"Hardly. Call your boss."

He smiled. "Sure." He pulled out his phone, arrogance pouring from his aura. This guy clearly wasn't hired for his brains.

"On speaker."

He shrugged, doing exactly as I requested. The phone rang once before someone picked up. "Is it done?" a cool

British voice asked.

Raoul raised a brow.

"That's not your boss," I said, hitting him upside the head with the butt of the gun. He collapsed with an *Oof,* the phone skidding across the floor. Sighing, I bent to retrieve the device.

"Sorry about that. Raoul decided to retire early." I slid the gun into my jacket to better hold the phone. "Taviv, is it?" I asked, taking him off speakerphone and pressing the device to my ear.

Silence.

"Ah, don't be shy. I've heard all about you from a mutual friend. Amara. She's not your biggest fan, you know." I knelt while I spoke, pulling out my blade. "Before I cut your buddy's throat, any final words?"

"Killian Bedivere," a new voice said, the throaty quality reminding me of a man who had smoked one too many cigars. How utterly cliché for a man in his position.

"Assad," I replied, drawing my knife across Raoul's skin. "I regret to inform you that tonight's business deal is about to go south. I hope you didn't need anything from those crime lords outside. One minute."

Setting the phone aside, I propped Raoul's dying

body up against the wood as a doorstop. It wouldn't necessarily halt someone else's entry, but it would give me time to address the issue should someone try to access the bathroom.

Standing, I turned on the sink to wash the blood from my dagger, preferring a clean tool to a soiled one.

Ah, bleach.

Useful.

Roughly two minutes later, my blade sparkled beneath the light. "Perfect." I returned the knife to its designated pocket and picked up the phone again. "Your associate made a mess I had to clean up. Where were we?"

"You were enlightening me on your desire to die."

My lips curled. "I do enjoy death, Assad. Thank you for noticing. Oh, while I have you, is there a particular way you would like me to take you out? Because I'm open to suggestions. Although, I should warn you, my counterpart has some pretty wicked ideas of her own on how to take you down."

Which was precisely the message I wanted to deliver. *Amara has told me everything.*

"You should be cautious of who you threaten, Mister Bedivere. Collateral damage is a very real complication. And with such a publicly known last name, it could put certain family members at risk. Your brother, for example, could be mistaken for you. You both have dark hair, yes? Similar stature, close in age. Where is he now? San Francisco?" A voice spoke up in the background. "I thought so, yes. That region of California is lovely this time of year."

"That's cute," I murmured, amused. "Good luck with your plans, Assad. Just know that I'll be seeing you soon." I dropped the phone and stomped on it, shattering it to pieces.

Goal accomplished.

And if he wanted to try to go after my brother, I wished him the utmost luck.

Only a Cavalieri could touch Hunter Bedivere, and Arthur would never accept the hit.

"You're making quite a mess," I said, looking down at a very dead Raoul. I tsked and nudged him aside with my foot.

We needed to go. And quickly.

I slipped out of the bathroom, thankful for the still-empty hallway, and returned to a ghostly white Amara.

"Time to go, kitten," I told her, pulling money from my pocket to toss onto the table. It was double the bill, which should satisfy the restaurant.

Until they found the body.

Fortunately, our reservations were under an untraceable alias.

Cav and Scarlet Dagger didn't exist.

Which meant I needed another alias. I could already picture Raven rolling her near-black eyes in response, causing me to smirk as I grabbed Amara's hand.

I thanked the host, tipping him generously on the way out, and pulled my trembling date into my side. "Shh," I murmured, my arm sliding around her shoulders. She didn't reply but kept pace with me as I guided her away from the restaurant and down the street.

Taking my phone from my pocket, I dialed a lift service first, requesting a pickup three blocks away. Then I called for a cleanup at the restaurant. Hopefully, they wouldn't have to burn it down.

As we neared the pickup point, I dialed my airline service and requested a departure from Cairo International for three hours from now. Even if the authorities caught wind of our aliases from the reservation list, it would take them days to pass the information through the systems.

We'd be long gone with a mysteriously lost destination.

Assuming Raven helped me out again.

Another long night ahead. Maybe this one would end with Amara naked and writhing in the plane. A man could dream.

AMARA

"He threatened your brother?" When I asked Killian about his conversation with Amir, that was the last thing I expected him to say. No, not true. He shocked me more by saying it would be fine. "How are you not worried?"

Killian chuckled as he settled into the executive chair beside me on the plane, his long legs sprawling in a casual way that boasted his relaxed state. "Hunter has one of the best security details in the world. And even if Amir manages to get through them, he then has to take my brother down. Which, believe me, won't be easy."

"Isn't he, like, a businessman?"

"Who has a penchant for martial arts and weapons, just like me." He grabbed my hand and brought it up to his lips, nibbling my thumb. "My brother can take

care of himself. Trust me."

"But you don't know what Amir is capable of," I pressed, not at all put at ease. "I've seen what he can do, Killian."

"Similarly, you don't know what my brother is capable of," he countered, smiling. "If it were me, would you be this concerned? Or should I be jealous?"

"That's not the point. You need to at least warn him."

"Already done, kitten. Would you like to hear his reply?"

"You told him about Amir?"

"I informed him that my recent work assignment mentioned him in passing." He released my hand to pull out his phone, scrolling. "Here's what he said." He showed me the screen.

Excellent. San Francisco is fucking boring. I could use the distraction.

"He sounds just like you," I admitted.

"Yeah, except he runs a billion-dollar corporation. Anyone who touches him is an idiot. I wish Assad luck in his endeavor." He pocketed his phone just as a flight attendant sauntered into the main cabin.

"Mister Bedivere," she greeted, her voice a sultry murmur. "Can I get either of you anything for takeoff?"

"Scotch on ice," he replied before glancing at me. "Anything for you, sweetheart?"

"Coffee." We just arrived in Cairo a few hours ago and were already leaving. I needed caffeine. A lot of it.

"Cream and sugar?" she asked in a tone that grated on my nerves.

Killian chuckled. "She prefers it black," he said before I could comment, his dark eyes finding mine. "Are you hungry?"

After our dinner experience? "No."

He considered me for a moment, then turned back to the flight attendant. "I'm in the mood for dessert. Can you prepare a sundae bar once we're in the air?"

Her expression lit up like he'd just asked her to marry him. "Oh, yes. Of course, sir." She whirled around, her ass swinging as she went, and disappeared.

"I think she's hoping you'll eat her with the sundae," I said, frowning after her. "Unless she's always this chipper?" A thought occurred to me then. "Is she your usual attendant?" The flight we took to Cairo was staffed by three men. No women.

Killian's lips twitched. "No. I've never met her. But the company I hire supplies all sorts of services, and she might be misinterpreting my needs for the night." He shrugged. "Doesn't matter. The sundae is for you."

"I said I wasn't hungry."

"I know." His gaze smoldered as he ran it over me. "It's for you, Amara."

My mouth went dry. "Oh" was all I could say.

He smirked and checked his phone as it buzzed. "Ah, perfect. Raven is working on our credentials. I knew she loved me." Then he laughed as an image came through.

"Is that a cat licking its ass?" I asked, squinting at his screen.

"Raven has a fucked-up sense of humor." He typed back a reply, then pressed a button on the console between us. "We're cleared for Charlotte."

"Thank you, sir" was the reply. "Just finished up the paperwork on our end. We should be in the air in about ten minutes."

"Excellent." He relaxed while I gaped at him.

"Charlotte?" My stomach twisted with the

mention of the too-familiar city. "What exactly did you promise Amir?" I unbuckled my seat belt, the need to bolt hitting me hard in the chest, tears filling my eyes. "I trusted you."

Oh God.

My lip wobbled, his image swimming before me.

"I trusted you," I repeated, furious and hurt all at the same time.

So stupid. I'd been *so incredibly stupid.*

My feet were already moving, my destination unknown.

But not to Charlotte.

Ever.

I refused.

No!

I should have known this would happen. Killian had lulled me into this sense of ease, convinced me he was helping me, just to take me back to *him.*

My name whipped through the air, but I was done listening. I needed to run. To escape. I couldn't go back, not now, not after everything.

The door was closed.

The stairs gone.

Could I jump?

I needed to get it open first, but the handle—

My back hit the wall, a fuming Killian in front of me. I didn't think. I reacted. My fist hit his jaw, my knee went upward and connected with his thigh. His curses were lost to the rushing of water in my ears, and then I found myself in the air. I kicked and wiggled and screamed and tried to slap him. Anything to get away from him and our future destination.

Charlotte.

Where he lived.

Hell.

I couldn't—*wouldn't*—go back there.

Tears streamed down my cheeks, the world shifting around me too quickly and words passing over my head. I didn't know what he said. Didn't care. Too consumed by my need to flee.

"You can't make me go back. You can't." I shook my head vigorously, compelling him to hear me. "No!" I tried to hit him again, but he threw me onto something soft. My wrists ended up shackled beneath one of his hands, his body holding mine down as he glowered at me from above.

"Fuck, Amara." The growl in his voice vibrated my chest, his thighs pinning mine to… to… a mattress?

Where the fuck are we?

I glanced around, noting the small bedroom fixtures, the lack of windows, the rumble beneath me.

"Sir, I—"

"It's fine. Tell them to take off. And shut the fucking door."

"Of course."

"No!" I shouted.

"Leave us. Now." His demand was followed by a snick that seemed to steal my breath, sealing my fate, encasing me in this room, on a plane, destined to return to my worst nightmare. I trembled, my insides crying out in pain and fear. Somehow this hurt more than him delivering me to Boris in Germany. Maybe because that never felt real.

But this…

This was happening.

And I couldn't do anything to stop it.

"Amara," Killian snapped.

But I didn't care what he had to say. He'd betrayed me in the worst way. I'd never trusted anyone before and foolishly made him my first. Because there'd been no other choice, no other way, but I allowed myself to get comfortable, to—

His mouth captured mine, rousing me from my mind.

What the hell?

No!

I started fighting in earnest, squirming beneath him, desperate to find a way out, but he was too strong, too *big*. His palm held my wrists with dangerous ease above my head, his opposite hand circling my throat as he lifted to glower down at me again.

"Stop," he demanded.

"Fuck you!"

"Jesus, Amara." The roar of the engines overpowered his voice, the vibrations as we picked up speed shattering something inside of me.

It's done.

I'm going back to him.

There's no option here.

I... I've lost.

My shoulders shook, my lungs begging me to breathe as I crumpled beneath him, all my fight gone.

He had me right where he wanted me.

Broken.

Alone.

Finished.

"Amara," he whispered, shifting to the side and gathering me in his arms. We were already in the air, the change in atmosphere causing my head to ache. Or maybe that was my heart. No, my entire body.

Oh, hell. I didn't know anything anymore. I'd never felt so *destroyed*. How had he managed to do this to me? People had played games with me all my life. None of them ever won.

Until Killian.

Why him?

Why did I have to trust him?

Because I *liked* him.

Because for the first time in my life, I actually desired someone. Every encounter until this point had been forced on me, except Killian.

But it was all a lie.

A fucked-up punishment.

A ruse meant to belittle me and remind me of my place.

"Charlotte is the last place he'll search for us," Killian said, his lips against my ear. "I know it's not somewhere you want to go again, but it's the safest location for us to hide. And there's a benefit this weekend with two of our marks in attendance. It's the perfect next step."

I blinked, startled and confused by his words. "Wh-what?"

He combed his fingers through my hair, his opposite arm wrapped tightly around my back.

"It's a masquerade gala." He kissed my temple and pulled back a little to gaze down at me. "I mentioned it earlier this week, remember?"

Did he? My head ached too much for me to recall the conversation. Too many plans. Too many details. Too much *pain*.

"I thought we'd still be in Cairo," he continued. "However, since Raoul essentially fell into our lap, it accelerates our timeline and makes the event on Friday night a possibility. We'll need to find a way onto the guest list, but I know a few people who can help with that. And I know somewhere we can lie low in Charlotte. Assad and Malcom will be too busy searching overseas for us to even consider our relocation to North Carolina. By the time they realize where we are, we'll already be into the next phase of our plan."

"You're...?" I swallowed, my throat sore from my emotional outburst. Had I screamed? Wept? I couldn't focus, too exhausted from all the weights holding me down.

Amir.

Malcom.

Clarissa.

I shuddered, wanting nothing more than to forget *everything*.

Except, Killian had no intention of returning me to them. This was part of his master plan. To take down Malcom and everyone else.

"You're not taking me back to him," I whispered, the words more for myself than for him.

"What?" Killian reared back as if I'd slapped him. Again, I supposed. Because I had hit him. A few times. And he never fought back, just picked me up and carried me here. "How could you possibly think that?"

"Charlotte..." The word had been a trigger, my

worst fear coming to life, and I'd reacted as a scared little girl. Like the time when I was sixteen and hid under my bed, shaking, refusing to believe my *parents* had allowed all those men to touch me.

"Amara." Killian gripped my hair, forcing my head back. "I've never lied to you. I will never lie to you. Yes, you were my mark. But I've since fired the client, rendering the project null and void. You're my new client, kitten. We're going to kill everyone who has ever touched you. Not because you're paying me. Not because I expect anything from you. But because I want to. Understand?"

Another round of stupid tears filled my eyes, this time for an entirely different reason—relief.

Relief tinged with wonder.

And maybe a little thrill.

"You're really helping me," I marveled, uncertain of how to interpret the emotions that came with the revelation.

Because I believed him. Maybe I shouldn't, maybe this was all just a ruse to calm me down, but his gaze radiated truth. As did all of his actions. He kept me in the loop. Told me what he was doing, even when delivering me to Boris. Continued to confide in me about his past and present. Had followed through with every action thus far without faltering.

Yet I'd doubted him now.

"I..." I swallowed the lump in my throat. "I'm not used to..."

"Shh." He brushed his lips over mine. "I know, Amara. It's okay. You have every right to doubt me and our situation. I'm a lot of things, but a coward isn't one of them. If I were taking you to Malcom, I would tell you."

Pride and honor gleamed in his molten chocolate irises, searing me from the inside out. God, this man had the power to destroy me in a way no one else ever had. The last several minutes proved that to me.

How could someone I'd known for such a brief amount of time possess that sort of talent?

What else could he make me feel?

Passion?

Excitement?

Pleasure?

I shivered at the thought, his nearness suddenly morphing into a new possibility. Not one tied to fear and emptiness, but to heat and potential. A life I wanted but never had an opportunity to consider. An ardor for the future.

My blood warmed at the prospect, my heart skipping a beat.

And his dilating pupils said he sensed it.

The change between us.

The need.

The intensity.

I palmed the side of his face, tracing his lips with my thumb. So soft. Perfect. Alluring. I wanted to taste him. Truly. Not a tease. Not a taunting moment. But a real, thorough, sensual kiss. Because I wanted him.

"Killian…" It was a request and a plea, my eyes seeking his, my body curving into his for an entirely new purpose. I craved comfort in a form I'd never experienced. Hot. Passionate. Solace.

His grip in my hair loosened, his hand sliding to the back of my neck. "Come here, kitten." He rolled to his back, guiding me with him. My legs straddled his hips as though they belonged there. "Take what you need."

How he knew, I couldn't say. I didn't care, too lost

in his words—his permission—to think beyond the moment. My lips took his with a fervor I unleashed with my tongue against his. And he accepted every stroke, every nip, every dominate sweep of his mouth. He allowed me to lead, giving me a power I never dreamed to be possible.

His strength coiled beneath mine, reminding me of a predator waiting to pounce, but his touch remained tender. My dress tangled around our legs, forcing me to adjust and pull the fabric up to my hips to resettle against him.

And ohhh, was that a mistake in the best way.

Because it left me completely bare against his dress pants.

No panties.

Just the thin wool of his trousers against my bare, wet pussy. I writhed against him, emotions mingling with a dark yearning inside me, begging to be unleashed. But I needed more than just a kiss and light petting.

The teasing all week, tonight, everything, had lit a fire inside of me that only he could extinguish. And that required the real Killian, the confident one who treated me as a fighter, a woman, not a fragile doll.

I cupped his face between my palms, lifting my lips from his. "Give me more. I'm done with the games. You need to follow through."

"Never been a game, sweetheart," he murmured, his grip on my neck tightening. "Seduction is an art." He flipped me to my back, settling between my thighs and rubbing his hard arousal against mine.

I moaned, arching into him, only to be pushed back down by his hand on my hip. His opposite palm moved to my throat, squeezing just enough to demonstrate his newfound control.

"Is this what you want, Amara?" A hint of darkness lurked in his tone, an ominous flare that had me swallowing, my mouth going dry.

"Yes," I breathed, knowing it to be true.

He squeezed more, cutting off my air supply. "Are you sure?"

My thighs clenched around his, my body reacting in the most fucked up of ways to his perceived violence. Because I trusted him not to truly hurt me. He could have done so many times before and didn't. Everything he did heightened the pleasure, intensifying the experience and leaving me panting for more.

So I nodded, unable to speak.

And gasped as he released me. His mouth sealed over mine, inhaling me, as if the exhale from my lips belonged to him and he wanted to savor it.

Then he kissed me.

Truly.

Harshly.

Beautifully.

His tongue reclaimed its throne, stealing the dominance right out from under me while expertly teaching me how to obey him again. Each stroke had me bowing in supplication, my body quivering with unrestrained sensuality.

The hand on my hip slid beneath my dress, his bare touch eliciting a hiss from deep within me. I threaded my fingers in his hair, holding him to me, begging him with my mouth to do more.

And by some measure of a miracle, he gave in to me.

His palm slid from my throat to my breast, cupping it through the fabric and tweaking my nipple. "I want you naked, kitten. Now." He knelt between my legs, forcing me to widen them to accommodate.

I gazed up at him beneath hooded eyes. "I want you naked, too."

He tsked, a knife somehow magically appearing in his hand.

Where does he keep those?

No, better question: What is he doing?

KILLIAN

Amara's gaze darkened with intrigue, her arousal an addictive scent. One I wanted to explore with my tongue. But she needed to let go, to lose herself to my touch, to remember it was me who knelt between her legs.

And I required her trust.

She went to her elbows, her gaze holding a demand that made me smile.

"I'm in charge now, sweetheart. Not you." I pressed the blade to her thigh, drawing the razor edge upward. She shivered, a tantalizing line of goose bumps trailing behind my sharp touch. "Do you like the danger, kitten? The very real prospect that I could accidentally—or purposely—slice your gorgeous skin?"

Her chest rose and fell, the rest of her remaining beautifully still. "You won't," she breathed.

"I won't?" I repeated, pressing the tip into her hip, right at the pressure point. "Are you sure about that?"

She licked her lips, her pupils flaring. "Do it." A dare. A provocation. A woman trying to top from the bottom.

I tsked again, sliding my dagger across her pelvis beneath the dress. "Are you wet for me, darling?"

"Yes," she hissed, her lips parting.

"Mmm..." I slipped the metal through her damp folds, the action hidden by the fabric of her dress. It'd pooled around her waist, with pieces hiding the part of her I wanted most.

So fucking hot.

It increased the risk, heightened the moment, and elicited a shudder from her that oozed temptation.

There was the trust I desired.

Even being taunting, my weapon pressed against her pretty cunt, she was aroused and wanting. My perfect partner. My beautiful Amara.

I leaned in to kiss the top of her thigh, thanking her for her faith in me. She moaned, my blade resting against her mound.

"Don't move," I whispered, licking a path upward,

beneath her dress.

"Killian…" Her head fell back, her arms shaking as she fought to hold her position up on her elbows.

So much discipline.

I adored it.

And she needed it.

Her episode before revealed a great deal about her headspace. She harbored an incredible amount of strength and a resolve I admired, but her past threatened her spirit. The panic in her gaze had chilled me to my very soul, calling on me to heal her, forcing me to engage her in this sexual game of limits. Because it was what she needed to let go, to move on, to work through the pain.

I understood her in a manner few others ever would. Maybe because I lived in a world of death and she flirted with the realm daily throughout her life. Maybe because we were meant to find each other. Maybe because we offered each other an escape from reality.

Regardless, her trust in me in this moment was an aphrodisiac that stirred a yearning inside me no one else had ever evoked.

And I wanted to reward her for it in every sensual way known to man.

I kissed her mound, shifting my knife and lifting to catch her eye. "I still want you naked, Amara. Sit up." She was still balancing on her elbows, her limbs strained from trying not to move.

But she did as I requested, her gaze heavy-lidded. She didn't wait, just pulled her dress up and over her head, then removed her bra with a twist and tossed it to the side.

The only things left were her shoes. I grabbed the right one, sliding the heel off before bending her knee and pressing her foot flat to the bed. She bit her lip as I repeated the action with her other leg, leaving her wide open and completely naked for my perusal.

"Gorgeous," I murmured, admiring every inch of her.

I'd hung up my jacket when we entered the jet, leaving me clad in my dress shirt and pants. Amara's heated gaze urged me to remove them, but I didn't.

No. I wanted to play. To tease. To worship her. To erase every second of harm and replace it with a memory worth remembering.

"If you don't do something—"

I leaned over and pressed the knife to her lips, arching a brow. "Patience, Amara."

She licked the metal in response, her gaze glowing with sensual intent. I nearly lost it right there, my desire to throw the dagger aside and fuck her causing my balls to tighten and my cock to throb.

"Fuck," I whispered.

"Patience is dull," she replied against my blade, her tongue drawing another wet path up the steel. "I'd prefer your cock, Killian."

"Oh, kitten." I tapped her on the nose with my knife and bent down to take her mouth, teaching her a lesson with my tongue. She groaned in response, her arms wrapping around my neck, but I pulled away, nipping her chin. "I'll feed you my cock, and by the time I'm done with you, you'll be begging me for a break."

"Promises, promises," she sighed, her cheeks flushed. "Just fuck me, Killian."

"No." I shifted back to my knees, drawing my blade down her neck as I moved, pausing at her nipples to circle one of the stiff tips. "Patience is not dull, darling." I pressed down, causing her to hiss, and bent to lick the tender scratch. "It's exciting," I whispered, laving her tit and sucking her taut peak into my mouth.

She arched into me, her restraint shattering.

I switched breasts, returning my knife to the sheath sewn into my pants pocket, and used my teeth to help her teeter on the balance of pleasure and pain.

Her reactions were exquisite, her head lolling to one side and then the other, my name a curse from her mouth. I loved it, having her completely at my mercy while being free to voice her own opinions and desires. A delicate dance between submission and dominance, that special place where trust and adoration ruled. I wouldn't trade it for anything in the world.

Amara required an experience adorned in ecstasy, and that was exactly what I intended to give her.

I kissed a path down her torso, pausing to dip my tongue in her belly button. She watched with a look of wonder as I continued my trail, my desired location clear, and her reaction told me she wasn't used to this—to being adored.

But that was exactly what I wanted.

She deserved to be worshiped and praised, and I

showed her that with my mouth against her clit.

"Oh God." She bowed off the bed, her response that of a woman experiencing true rapture for the first time. Of all the things done to her body, this had clearly not been one of them. Or perhaps it'd been too long.

Her fingers threaded through my hair, giving me a tug and pressing me closer at the same time, as if she couldn't decide if she wanted me to stop or to never stop. I nibbled gently on her sensitive little nub, just enough to provide her with the mix of sensation she required.

Amara rewarded me with a long moan, my name never sounding more perfect. I slid one finger inside her, testing her strength and stamina, then added a second when I felt her pulse around me.

So close.

Her body was strung like a bow, begging to be mastered and played.

And I gave her what she needed, my tongue matching my inner strokes, her body falling apart to my tune.

She screamed, her lower body quaking with her

eruption, her hand fisting my hair as though needing to hold on to something while she floated to the heavens and back. I smiled against her, nowhere near done.

I needed to hear that again.

Right now.

She squirmed in protest, the pleasure too much, but I pushed her through it, knowing she could handle it, knowing she *needed* it. The best kind of torment. A torture every woman should endure.

And oh, how Amara endured it.

"Killian," she pleaded, weeping, her beautiful mouth parted on a pant lost to the roar of the engines outside. But I could feel her convulsing, her euphoria sweet on my tongue. She came apart a second time, her nails digging into my scalp.

I grinned, debating a third time when she yanked sharply at my hair, her thighs quivering around me.

"Too much?" I asked, my lips brushing her swollen clit.

"I… I want…" She shuddered, her head falling back again, her lips parting on a groan. "*Fuck.*"

"Is that a request, sweetheart?" I chuckled against

her damp flesh, giving her another long, thorough lick before sliding off the bed.

She whimpered, her hands reaching blindly for me. I caught one and brought it to my lips, nipping the pad of her finger. "You still owe me a blow job, kitten." *Preferably one without the needle-jabbing climax.*

Her smoky eyes lifted to mine, intrigue dilating her pupils. I unbuttoned my shirt while she watched, slowly revealing myself to her devilish gaze. Appreciation colored her features, mingling with the afterglow of her orgasms and painting the most erotic portrait I'd ever seen.

Long lashes, plump lips, flushed cheeks, and an anticipatory gleam that had my cock pulsing against my zipper.

"Take off my pants," I told her, needing her hands on me.

She crawled to the edge of the bed, far too slowly, and went to her knees before me. Her lips pressed against mine while her hands went to my belt. No arguments. No comments. Just pure compliance, and it was sexy as hell.

I returned her kiss while I finished removing

my shirt, then fisted my hand in her thick hair. Her nimble fingers unfastened my pants, unfaltering, her actions trained. The wool loosened around my hips, falling to my thighs as she pushed them down. I kicked them off, along with my shoes, and slid my grip to the back of her neck.

She palmed me through my boxer briefs, her touch searing and not nearly enough. "Boxers, too," I urged against her mouth.

"Yes, sir." She sucked on my lip, her nails scraping across my lower abdomen. And then she did exactly as I requested, freeing my cock and guiding the fabric down my legs.

She pressed against me, her body hot and needy, a purr tickling her throat. Her nickname—one I'd never assigned to anyone else—couldn't be more perfect. She really was a feisty kitten. And I fucking loved it.

"Do you want me to kneel on the floor?" she asked, her mouth hot against mine. "Or in another position?"

My grasp around her nape tightened, the questions undoing something inside me. Her supplication was a gift, but I no longer wanted to fuck her mouth. I wanted to fuck *her*. To make this a joint experience, not a solitary one. This would be the night she remembered for years to come, the one she'd recall when she pleasured herself.

I wanted her to dream of me.

Indefinitely.

"Lie down." I released her, bending to remove my socks and to find the strip of condoms in my wallet. Her auburn strands fanned out around her as she sprawled out on the bed, her come-hither expression making my lips curl. "Vixen."

"Assassin," she countered.

I crawled over her, nuzzling her nose. "I prefer when you called me s*ir*."

She nipped my lower lip. "I'm wet for you, sir."

"Needy little minx."

Her eyebrow arched. "Talkative procrastinator."

"Keep insulting me," I murmured, rolling the condom on slowly, enjoying the taunting nature between us. "See what happens."

"Nothing, apparently." She hooked her calf around the back of my thigh. "You just keep speaking."

"Yeah?" I grabbed her hip. "You want something,

kitten?"

"You know what I want."

I angled her upward, aligning my cock with her entrance. "Say it."

She shivered, her nipples hard points calling for my mouth, but I was too consumed with her lips, needing to hear the words. Consent mattered here more than ever.

Her blue-green irises smoldered, her nails biting into my back. She smiled with a feline grace, the words leaving her eyes before her mouth. "Fuck me, Killian."

I slid home, her tight sheath eliciting a growl from my chest that paled in comparison to her groan.

Heaven.

That was what it felt like between her legs.

And I wanted to stay there forever.

Her hips rose to meet mine, her pelvis setting a pace before I could even start, but I met her full-on, taking over the rhythm and branding my name into her flesh.

My tongue gyrated with hers, establishing a passionate embrace accentuated by moans and delicious screams. She scratched her initials into my skin while I punctuated mine between her legs, and we engaged in a euphoric dance unlike any other of this world.

Amara was quite literally my queen.

And I her king.

Equals, but not. She mastered me in ways I never expected, just as I brought her to heel beneath me, guiding her body as if it were my own.

I craved more.

Yearned to do this all night. All week. All month. Forevermore.

Fuck, she was an addiction.

One I never intended to quit.

"More," she whispered, her legs wrapping around my hips. "I need more, Killian."

"I know." I silenced her with another kiss, driving into her with a force that would hurt most women, but not Amara. She accepted each thrust with one of her own, agony mingling with rapture. It intensified as I sat up, bringing her with me. She straddled my thighs, her back arching on a moan, her hips moving with a speed and endurance I admired. I grabbed her ass, forcing her to take more, each punishing drive eliciting sounds from her that spurred me onward. Her walls began to quiver, her body on the edge of a dangerous explosion that I longed to experience because I knew it would take me over with her.

"Let go, Amara." I pressed my lips to her throat, loving the way her pulse thundered against my tongue. "Come for me, kitten. Let me hear you roar."

She whimpered, her body denying her the impact she deserved.

I captured her mouth again, my hands wandering over her, petting her, reminding her of whose cock she rode, who held her. Each stroke eased her back to me, her heat evolving into a volcanic combustion that threatened to tip me over the edge, but I refused to go without her.

Easing her back onto the mattress, I slowed our movements just enough to adore her properly, to join us together in a sea of blissful sensation. She moaned, her pussy clenching around me, her panting hot against my lips.

And then she erupted, her scream excruciatingly beautiful.

"*Fuck*," I whispered, her cunt so damn tight. Two

more strokes had me falling with her, violent spasms rocking me harder into her and ripping a growl from my throat. It physically *hurt* to come this hard, leaving me empty and replete and shaking above her.

And yet I wanted more.

Another round.

A different position.

An entire night of exploration.

Amara had awoken a beast inside me, and that beast required surrender. *Her* surrender. Over and over and over again. Until I worked her out of my system.

Except I knew that would never happen. She'd slain me. Well and truly. From the inside out. I was done.

Possessed.

Destroyed.

Reborn.

Amara Rose was no longer a job. She wasn't even a client.

She'd just become my lover. And fuck if I wanted to fight it.

The woman was made for me. Just as I was made for her.

She's mine.

And anyone who tried to take her from me would die.

AMARA

"Are you sore, kitten?" Killian murmured, his lips against my ear as he thrust into me from behind.

"God, you're insatiable," I moaned, pressing back into him to provide deeper access.

Five days in Charlotte and he woke me up in a similar manner every morning—with either his cock between my thighs, or his tongue. And damn, I couldn't deny him. I needed this just as badly as he did. Craved it. Adored it.

He trailed kisses along my neck, sending a shiver of longing down my spine.

After this would be breakfast, then training. That'd become our routine. He wanted me to be comfortable with weapons, specifically guns. But he taught me a few things about knives, too. Mostly how to disarm someone and toss the blade away.

Granted, every time I tried a move on him, I failed.

He was just too damn fast and strong and *big*.

Just like his dick.

Seriously, the man embodied perfection. He had muscles in places I didn't know existed on a man, and he used every lean, sinewy inch to his advantage. Both in sparring and in the bedroom.

Always carrying a hint of pain underlined in an ecstasy I'd only ever experienced in his arms.

Hard.

Fast.

Thorough.

"Killian," I breathed, my orgasm mounting. He bit my pulse, yanking me backward with the sharp sting of his teeth. Then shoving me forward with a thrust I felt in my throat. He created a dichotomy within me that I didn't know how to handle. It erased all thought, forced me to remain focused on him, the moment, our connection, *this*.

I shuddered, my body moving to his command, my nipples throbbing, my clit begging. And as if he heard me, he slid his hand from my hip to the place I needed him most, and played me with expert skill.

I shattered around him, stars blinking behind my eyes and sending me to a plane of existence not of this world.

Every. Fucking. Time.

Part of me expected the sensation to diminish, to grow used to this insanity, but each experience with him felt brand new with a touch of old. As if we'd always done this. As though we were re-created for one another, our spirits intertwined for all of eternity.

I'd never believed in soul mates.

But something about Killian had me wanting to reconsider.

It terrified and thrilled me.

He had awoken a part of me I didn't know existed, and I adored him for it.

Killian gave me hope.

His arm locked around me as he shook through his own release, his mouth a brand against my shoulder. I sighed in contentment, stretching my legs and arms, causing him to chuckle against my neck. He slowly pulled out of me, then rolled off the bed to dispose of the condom. We'd already had the dreaded disease talk. Both of us were clean, and my IUD prevented pregnancy, but we favored safety. Or at least Killian did. I couldn't seem to think straight in his presence.

He scooped me into his arms, causing me to laugh as he carried me into the oversized shower of the guest suite. His friend's home offered the most modern and up-to-date styles in interior design. However, I'd yet to meet him. Apparently, *Powell*, as Killian called him, owned properties all over the world. This was just one of many.

The water felt like heaven against my shoulders, my feet finding the tiled floor as Killian lowered me. His hands were everywhere, memorizing my skin, my hair, my breasts. I laughed, feeling more rejuvenated than ever as we teased each other in the shower.

This life was one I could become accustomed to, even if it would be short-lived. But we had several names left on our target list.

Two of which would be removed tonight.

At the Hamptons' Masquerade Gala.

My stomach soured at the thought as Killian bundled me up in a towel.

Jefferson Hampton was evil encased in an expensive suit and adorned with a charming smile. Just picturing him gave me the chills.

"Where has your mind wandered?" Killian asked, tilting my chin upward, his brown eyes glimmering with knowledge.

It amazed me how well he could read me. His profession certainly helped, but our connection solidified his understanding. It allowed him a glimpse within my walls that no one had ever touched. A gift brought on by trust.

I palmed his cheek and lifted my lips to his, needing to taste him, to remind myself to enjoy the moment and not think too much beyond what it all meant. Just live in the here and now and not consider forever.

If this was all the happiness fate ever brought me, I'd accept it.

Just the glimpse of hope I needed to live.

His tongue slid into my mouth to engage mine in a lazy dance we'd mastered over the last week. My knees parted as he stepped between my thighs, my body already on fire for him again.

Maybe we were both insatiable.

He lifted me against him, his cock hard against my

slick folds. I wrapped my legs around his waist, more than ready to—

Killian's phone sounded from the other room, an alert that had me freezing against him because it sounded important.

"Malcom's on the move," he murmured, setting me back on the counter. He wandered off—naked—into the main bedroom area and returned a moment later with his phone in one hand, his tablet in the other.

The grin he wore put me at ease.

"He took the bait." He showed me the screen depicting a flight path. "He's on a plane to Madrid right now."

"What bait?" I asked.

"Oh, I had Raven make it look like we're in Spain by fussing with customs and immigration. I wanted to get Malcom away from the event tonight so we can proceed without any potential complications." He set both devices down on the counter and placed his palms on the marble beside my hips, caging me in with his gorgeous, hard body. "It'll be just me, you, and a few dead bodies. The perfect date."

I arched an eyebrow, darkly intrigued. "Sounds a

bit bloody for a date."

"No blood." He smiled, the look positively devilish on his striking features. "We'll poison them with the same concoction Malcom made you use on his adversaries."

"But I don't know what he gave me."

"Which is why I had Raven dig up the coroner reports."

My stomach churned for an entirely different reason than before. "I'm starting to wonder about this Raven," I admitted. He seemed to talk to her a lot.

Not that I had any reason to care about it.

Yet part of me wondered at their history and the easy camaraderie between them.

Did he play with her the way he did with me?

Hmm, no. He said they were only friends, that he wouldn't jeopardize their working relationship by fucking her.

But what if he secretly wanted to? And the only reason he didn't act on it was because of their business partnership?

Should the prospect of it bother me? Because it sort of did.

No, it really did.

Killian cupped my cheek, brushing his thumb over my bottom lip. "She's just a friend, kitten. No need for claws." He pressed his mouth to mine, gentle and coaxing. "I don't mix business and pleasure. Except with you."

"Why?" I asked, wrapping my palm around the back of his neck. "Why break the rules with me?"

"Because I want you," he whispered, gripping my hips. "Because you're mine."

"Am I?" The words were a breath against his mouth. "For how long?"

"Until you say otherwise." He kissed me hard, his hand fisting in my hair to tilt me back to his preferred angle. Always in charge. Always commanding. Always so fucking perfect.

I scratched my nails down his back, my way of signaling approval, and melted against him.

Because you're mine. Until you say otherwise.

Mmm, I rather liked the sound of that. "What if I want you to keep me forever?" I wondered out loud, teasing.

He licked the seam of my mouth, his gaze radiating

sin. "You'll have no arguments from me, as it'll take a lifetime to tame you anyway."

"That's quite a commitment. I thought you were married to your job?"

"Maybe I'm looking for a mistress." He nipped my lower lip. "You suit well for the part."

"Two weeks and we're already discussing affairs."

"I'm thorough," he murmured, smiling. "And when I take on a task, I commit."

"So I'm a task now?"

"You're certainly something." He tugged me to the edge of the counter, forcing my legs to wrap around him again. "Enough foreplay. I want to fuck you again before we go over the goals for tonight."

I tsked. "So demanding."

"Careful or it'll be your mouth I'm fucking, sweetheart." The threat caused my toes to curl. I adored his crude statements, especially when uttered as commands.

"That sounds tempting," I admitted, licking my lips.

"Then get on your knees, Amara."

I smiled, pushing him backward to make room for

me to stand. "Yes, sir."

Killian's palm burned against my lower back, his presence a steady confidence at my side as we entered the Hamptons' ballroom.

The plan was simple—intrigue, assassinate, leave.

All I needed to do was identify our targets, then Killian would take over from there. I'd provided him with a few pointers, little things I picked up on that Malcom did at events when he sold me to interested parties. Killian intended to mimic those actions, as well as the payment scheme his friend Raven had identified.

It'd be an intense evening, but it would end with the lethal items in my purse.

Because I wanted to kill these bastards. It was a realization that struck me this afternoon while discussing our options.

Jefferson Hampton had been there the night Malcom brutally took my virginity. He'd then requested my services several times over the horrible months that followed, his dark inclinations consistently painful.

The man embodied the devil.

As did his buddy Edward Franklin.

Malcom forced me to entertain the three of them on various occasions. At the same time.

I shivered, bile sliding up my throat at the unwelcome memories. They would forever haunt my nightmares. Their salacious grins, sweaty bodies, bulbous—

A light stroke up my spine drew my focus upward to Killian, his black-and-white mask hiding his face while highlighting the browns in his irises. His lips quirked at the side as he bent to kiss me softly. He drew his mouth across my cheekbone, beneath my ebony mask, to my ear. "You all right, kitten?"

I nodded. "Just remembering why I'm here." *To destroy my past and give myself a future.*

Clarissa and Geoff shattered my views on morals as an adolescent. They stole my innocence and created a temptress in high-society clothes.

Then Malcom taught me how to hate. How to fight. How to kill.

Now I would use my knowledge and history against them all.

Tonight would be the first step in taking control of my fate and giving me the tools I required to move on.

Killian had understood all of that and agreed to let me be the one to do it. His employer—Arthur—had sanctioned the kills, saying something about the bounties being acceptable. However, he believed Killian to be the executioner. I didn't care. I didn't want the money. I wanted vengeance for what was done to me.

I craved a dance with revenge.

"You're ready," Killian murmured, approval in his voice. "Let's wander and show off your dress."

His palm returned to my lower back, guiding me forward along the dance floor. Everyone stood talking and socializing over drinks, the majority oblivious to the dark undertones lurking inside this mansion.

The Hampton family put on a beautiful charade, benefiting charities and raising money for their favorite politicians. Jefferson was one of Malcom's oldest friends, having attended school together as boys. They'd formed a sick bond over their preferences in the bedrooms. Edward was the third of their fucked-up trio.

What did they enjoy? Sharing women. Violently.

I'd never met Jefferson's wife, but Malcom had suggested I would one day in an intimate setting. Something told me she would not miss her husband after I dispatched him.

Edward was single.

That made his assassination easier.

Of course, both were respected members of society. We had to play this right to avoid suspicion, mostly because Killian had borrowed his friend's identity for tonight's event.

Clayton Powell, the man who owned the house we'd taken refuge in this week, had received an invite to the Hamptons' Masquerade Gala. As Killian explained it, Clayton ran in similar circles but typically avoided functions such as this, preferring the ones with alcohol and younger attendees.

Killian described his friend as a playboy with a trust fund who preferred a good time over a dull one. When I asked how they knew each other, Killian merely smiled and said, "Work." I doubt Clayton was a Cavalieri, but didn't care enough to press. If it mattered, Killian would have elaborated.

Several attendees eyed us as we moved, most of the men admiring the low neckline of my dress. It dipped to my belly button, providing an indecent display of cleavage that marked me as an escort more than a date.

Which was entirely the point.

I needed to grab Jefferson's and Edward's attention, to entice them into bidding on me with Killian, and lure them away from the ballroom.

Then kill them.

My only disappointment was the lack of pain involved with dying by poison. They deserved worse. Like a knife across the throat. But Killian assured me this would send a deeper message, one Malcom would receive loud and clear. And I agreed.

"There," I said, spotting the familiar duo. I didn't point, just gestured subtly with my head as I moved to face Killian. He wrapped his palm around the back of my neck to pull me to him, staking his claim.

"You recognize them with the masks?" He murmured the words against my lips.

"It's their postures." Arrogant. Strong shoulders. Carved chins. Handsome men, as most in Malcom's circle were, but I recognized the monsters beneath their clothes now. I knew how to read a man with a glance alone.

It was why I trusted Killian. Yes, a predator writhed beneath his skin, but it was more akin to a panther lying in wait. The two bastards beside the ballroom wall reminded me of hyenas—desperate creatures that enjoyed ripping apart their prey while chattering happily about each detail.

A chill swept over me as I recalled their hands on me. Their tongues. Their cocks.

Killian's grip tightened, his gaze burning into mine. "Harness the pain and fury." His thumb traced my pulse. "It's your greatest weapon. Sharpen it into a lethal point and use it."

"Is that what you do?" I wondered, searching his features, or what I could see of them beyond the mask. "You don't strike me as having a harsh past."

"I don't." He skimmed his lips across my cheek, pressing them to my ear. "But I like to deliver pain. The kill excites me, kitten. Correcting a wrong, teaching someone a lesson, it's all a high that I crave." He nipped my earlobe. "Remember what I told you? I'm not a hero. I'm a villain and this is my playground."

My throat went dry at his words, my heart skipping a beat. "You're not a villain," I whispered, drawing my fingertips across his jaw. "Not to me." I'd been around my share of bad men. Killian didn't qualify.

His touch slid down to my backside, pulling me against him. "We're attracting attention."

"I thought that was the point." My lips curled into the most salacious grin I could muster—something he inspired all too easily from me. "Shall I go play?"

"Yes. Go mingle." He squeezed my ass. "Make them want you."

"Shouldn't be too hard," I murmured, sliding my nail into his mouth teasingly. "You picked the perfect dress." It was black and revealing and better designed for the bedroom than the ballroom.

He bit my finger, his gaze smoldering. It released with a pop that I heard over the subtle background music. "You wear it very well, darling."

"I know." I'd been bred and trained to pull off this gown, the low neckline and nonexistent back radiating sin and temptation. "I'm going to find someone to fix me a drink. Watch me?"

Those last two words slipped out as a plea, one I

didn't mean to voice but had to say. *Don't leave me.*
When had I ever relied on a man like this? On anyone?
Never. Yet somehow Killian had become my knight.
Not a white one, but a knight adorned in shades of
gray.

My assassin.

"As if I could look anywhere else." He winked as
he pulled away. "Give me something fun to watch,
kitten. Visual foreplay, if you will."

"I thought you preferred words?" I teased, my
blood warming despite the coolness left behind from
his lack of touch.

"Tonight, I'm in the mood for violence." His
expression darkened, the innuendo clear. He'd gone
easy on me this week, introducing me to his preferences
slowly and thoroughly, but tonight the panther inside
of him yearned to be freed.

And I was his desired prey.

I shivered, not in fear but in anticipation. "Then I
better get to work, sir."

"Now," he said, the command in his voice one that
caused my lips to quirk upward. It would be so easy to
defy him, but I didn't want to.

No, quite the opposite.

I wanted to impress him, and in doing so, impress myself.

Because we were a team.

And tonight we would cement our partnership in blood.

KILLIAN

Amara owned the room, her dress one of the more scandalous in attendance. Women watched her with envy, men with desire.

I observed her with the knowledge that she'd be coming home with me tonight. That I would be the one to undress her. To fuck her. To claim her. And knowing all that stirred something inside of me. A possessive instinct, one that burned through my veins and tightened my stomach.

These sensations were new and volatile and entirely too welcome.

When Arthur gave me the go-ahead to take out these marks, I couldn't tell him the truth of why I wanted them dead. Not that he'd asked, but it still felt like an omission. Especially as Amara would be the assassin on this case.

The Cavalieri Della Morte prided themselves on secrecy, on not letting anyone from the outside world know our true nature. Yet I'd confided almost my entire history to Amara. Fuck, this was an even deeper initiation into my dark life, ingraining her in my sins and cementing her place at my side.

It was wrong.

It felt right.

It was likely a mistake.

But I didn't care.

She'd become the mistress to my work, creating a bond I never knew I wanted. And watching her work now was an experience that made it all worthwhile.

Men approached from all angles, begging for a second glance despite the women on their arms. It amused me and disgusted me. I couldn't take my eyes off Amara long enough to admire anyone else in attendance. None of them mattered anyway. She was the only one in this room that I desired.

Our targets remained a steady presence in my peripheral vision. While they'd definitely noticed Amara, they clearly didn't recognize her. The mask helped, as did her revealing gown. It drew their focus to her assets, not her face. And while I'd gathered they were intimately familiar with her body, they obviously hadn't worshiped it like I had. Otherwise, they would have identified her right away.

Amara tilted her head back on a laugh that had my lips twitching and several heads turning. She certainly knew how to work a room. Was that part of her training? Or a natural skill? Regardless, I adored it.

As did our quarries.

I casually checked my watch. An hour had passed, leaving my hands aching for Amara's curves. The sooner we ended this, the sooner I'd have her naked beneath me. Best to move this along, then.

Catching Amara's eye, I gave her a nod of my head that she returned while Franklin and Hampton observed. Lifting my hand, I gave her another signal with two of my fingers, one she told me to use. Apparently, it meant something in her former world. She responded with another nod before lifting her drink in salute and returning to the male at her side with a smile.

I forced a smirk before checking my phone, all part of our plan.

From my peripheral vision, I caught Franklin and Hampton shifting, their interest definitely piqued. Pretending not to notice, I scrolled through a few messages from Nikolai.

Thanks for the date night idea, Dagger. We had a bloody good time.

Now my lips really did pull into a grin. Nikolai was Russian, not English. Which meant he literally had a *bloody* good time. *Nothing like a sharp edge to darken the evening,* I typed back.

Dots appeared, Nikolai having obviously been waiting for my acknowledgment. *Too true. Unfortunately, our double date didn't last very long. They couldn't seem to handle my pchelka's penchant for shiny toys.*

Pity, I replied. *Clearly, they didn't understand the beauty of her skills.* I'd not seen Nikolai's female in action, but from what I knew about her, she'd be a formidable adversary with a blade. Amara would adore her. Perhaps we could go on a proper double date someday, not dual nights of killing sprees.

Definitely not. Feel free to send more date ideas, if you have them.

I chuckled. *Noted. Thanks again.*

Anytime.

With a swipe of my finger, I checked the most recent update from Raven regarding Malcom's whereabouts. Still in Europe. Excellent.

Movement out of the corner of my eye had me switching my screen to another text, one about purchasing agreements. It was a manufactured message I asked Raven to send me from a fake number.

The clearing of a throat had me glancing upward without bothering to hide my phone. Franklin took the opportunity to not-so-discreetly read the words on the screen while Hampton focused on me.

"I don't believe we've met," he said, his voice holding a pompous edge to it that had me wanting to punch him. But I smiled instead.

"Clayton Powell." I extended my hand, fully aware that my buddy Powell had never met this douchebag despite receiving numerous invites to his charity events. It wasn't Clayton's scene. He preferred parties with alcohol and available women, mostly to keep up his charade as a playboy heir. I'd discovered the truth about him years ago. Very few had caught on since, making his presence on the scene lucrative indeed.

"Clayton Powell?" Hampton repeated, his light-colored eyebrows rising above his black mask. "Why, I never thought I'd see the day where you accepted one of my invites."

I lifted a shoulder. "I was in town and bored." I pretended to remember my phone. "Oh, sorry, one minute." I typed back a bogus reply of acceptance while both men watched, then slid the device into my jacket pocket. "Minor business deal."

"How much is she worth?" Franklin asked, surprising me with his boldness.

I made a show of feigning confusion. "I'm sorry?" Powell would never purchase a woman for sex and would likely hate me for implying otherwise under his name, but I had no choice. Besides, these two jackasses would be dead come morning. So no harm done, really.

Or maybe I owed my buddy a bourbon. Top shelf. No, a case of it.

I noted it for later and refocused on the two males before me, who claimed to be upstanding citizens of society. One was married, for fuck's sake. But God only knew where he'd left his wife for the evening. As

I didn't know what she looked like, I couldn't exactly identify her in the sea of masquerade attire.

"I'm not sure what you mean," I added when they both just kept staring at me.

"Don't play coy." Franklin's lips curled into what could only be described as a salacious grin. "How much is the girl worth for a night?"

"And who are you?" I asked, adding an edge to my tone the way Powell would. He'd never met these men, nor would he consider them anyone worth recognizing. And he'd make sure they knew that in the same manner I was doing now.

Franklin held out his hand. "Edward Franklin."

I ignored him and refocused on the taller douchebag beside him. "And you?"

His hazel eyes narrowed through the pinholes of his mask, clearly not a fan of my perceived lack of knowledge. *Tough shit, asshole.*

"Jefferson Hampton," he replied flatly.

He sounded so arrogant that I couldn't help baiting him. "Ah, you're the one I have to thank for this decidedly boring affair." I searched for Amara, or pretended to, anyway. I knew exactly where she was because I'd kept her within my line of sight. "Well, not completely boring," I added, grinning in anticipation of the night ahead.

"She's exquisite," Franklin murmured, following my gaze. "Which brings me back to the original question. How much for a night?"

Oh, not much. Your death will do, I thought, purposely not acknowledging him.

Amara had told me about this part of her world— the one initiated by mere hand gestures and texts with account numbers and figures.

I always knew this cruelty existed, but had no idea how easily it was conducted right under the nose of society. No one around us even acknowledged the conversation, blissfully unaware of the two men before me requesting to buy a night with my date as if she were an object, not a person.

That they felt confident enough to approach me in this room suggested this wasn't their first time, either. Which, of course, I knew. These men had touched Amara. Intimately. More than once, from what I'd gathered, and her adverse reaction upon noticing them confirmed they hadn't been kind to her.

Poison seemed too humane for their heinous activities. A night beneath my blade would be far more fitting.

"Perhaps he's not as interested in sharing as we thought," Hampton said when I didn't reply. "Newbies don't always understand the signals, after all."

"Newbie?" I repeated with a laugh, forcing myself to look at him. "If anyone is new here, it's you. Asking me for a night with her? As if you stand a chance at paying my price." I tsked. "You have no idea who you're dealing with, gentlemen. That woman is out of your league." I meant every word but softened it with a smile. "However, if you have an offer, I'm open to hearing it. Although, I've already received two others for the night, and they were quite high." Which Franklin would already know because he'd blatantly read the text from my phone.

"So you admit she's for sale," Franklin said, his eager energy making me sick to my stomach.

"Everything has a price," I admitted. This one would just cost him his life. No big deal.

"We'll triple your highest offer if you let us share her. No rules." Franklin uttered the words with the confidence of a male used to buying what he wanted, how he wanted.

I arched a brow. "You don't even know my highest offer." A complete lie. He'd read the price off my phone, but I didn't want him to know I'd seen him do it because then it would be obvious that I left the screen in his view on purpose.

Hampton surprised me by replying, "We can afford it."

"Can you?" I glanced between them, allowing them to see my false intrigue. Then I quoted a number higher than the value Franklin would have read, just to show him I was playing hardball.

"Not an issue," Hampton assured me.

I studied them both as if considering their offer. "I have two rules," I said, earning me a scowl from Franklin. "First, I always watch. Second, if what you're doing interests me, I get to play, too. She's mine, after all."

Franklin's scowl shifted into a smile that chilled my insides. "We accept those terms."

Of course they would. Amara hadn't gone into much detail, but from what I gathered, Malcom favored group play. And he considered these two bastards his best friends.

I refused to think about what they did to her. Not yet. Not until I had them alone.

"When?" I asked, needing to move this along before I accidentally stabbed one of them.

"Preferably sooner rather than later, as we're paying for the entire night." Hampton sounded so nonchalant, as if he hadn't just purchased a woman for the evening. Did he think she was willing? Did he care?

"Won't you be missed?" I wondered out loud, glancing around. "This is your event, isn't it?"

"My wife plans it all," he replied, shrugging. "She'll handle it in my absence."

I nodded because I had no words for that. Nothing kind, anyway. How often did he leave his *wife* to host while he fucked another woman? Perhaps she didn't care, preferring the night away from him.

What a sick and twisted life he led.

Franklin, too.

Ending them would be a favor to humanity.

I cleared my throat. "We can proceed with the transaction. I require the funds first."

Franklin pulled out his phone. "Tell me your details."

I gave him an account Raven had set up for this purpose. "Where do want your evening entertainment?" I asked after checking my phone to see that the amount was fully transferred. I forwarded the confirmation to Raven. She could play with the funds as she saw fit. A reward for her help, one I knew she'd balk at, but she deserved the payment regardless.

"There's a room designed for this in the other wing." He gave me directions on the desired location for our meeting.

"We'll be there in fifteen minutes." I started to walk away, when Franklin caught my arm.

"Just to be clear, we prefer to do the unwrapping," he advised, his voice low.

Not going to happen. "Of course." I forced a smile and gave them a nod, unable to say a proper goodbye. My attention was on Amara and preparing her for the final task of the evening.

Poison was no longer good enough.

I'd wanted to send a message.

Well, we'd be sending one all right.

I joined Amara at the bar, taking her elbow and cutting off her conversation with the man beside her. "Are you done playing, kitten?" I asked against her ear.

She smiled. "Forgive me, Congressman. My date has finally returned."

"In my day, a man never left his date unattended for long. You never knew what kind of scoundrel might creep in, you see," the older male beside her said, his tone kinder than I would have expected. "It was lovely to meet you, Ms. Dagger."

"The pleasure was all mine." She gave him an alluring smile, her eyes sparkling through her mask.

"You take good care of this one, son. She's special." He patted me on the shoulder as if we were old friends, leaving me a little befuddled by his camaraderie.

But as I agreed with his sentiment, I replied, "Of course, sir."

"Good." He nodded, satisfied, and wandered off.

"Interesting company you keep," I said, watching the bald man amble away.

"He's probably one of the few decent men in the room." She slid off her stool, grabbing her purse. "I've always liked him."

"You've met before?"

She shrugged, walking alongside me as I escorted her toward the exit. "In passing."

Shit. "Did he recognize you?"

"If he did, he kept the detail to himself."

I noted the information as something to research later. Amara couldn't be tied to this event at all, especially after what we planned to do. If that meant I needed to silence the old congressman—kind or not—I would. Keeping her record clean mattered first and foremost.

My phone buzzed as we exited the ballroom. Seeing Raven's name on the ID had me answering it. "Yes?"

"Stop sending me money."

I smirked. "You're welcome, darling."

"Dick." Typing sounded in the background. "I'm donating it to an organization in Atlanta that helps trafficking victims."

"Good." I gestured down a hallway to our left with my chin, my hands otherwise preoccupied between holding the phone and touching Amara's back. She turned without a word, her expression grim. "Did you call for my approval? Because you know it's granted."

"As if anything I do requires your approval," she retorted, causing me to grin.

"Then why are you calling?" I prompted. She knew my plans with Amara for the evening, which meant she'd phoned me for more than just a complaint about the money.

"You know that thing you had me researching in Boston?"

"I do, yes." She meant the auction circuit Clarissa and Geoff Rose ran.

"I just got a hit on something happening next weekend."

"Send me the details."

"I will, but, K, you need to be careful. These people are bad news, dude."

My lips twitched, amused. Her concern was quite touching. "Don't worry, little bird. I can handle myself."

She snorted. "Yeah, yeah. Sending details now. But don't say I didn't warn you."

The line went dead, causing me to chuckle as I returned the phone to my pocket.

"Little bird?" Amara repeated, a frown in her voice.

"A play on her code name." One Raven hated. I glanced up and down the empty corridor Hampton had described, searching for cameras and finding none. Never a good sign in a home this large. It meant the owner didn't want security guarding it. "Have you been here before?"

Amara nodded, her bottom lip catching between her teeth. She turned at the end of the hallway, following the path Hampton had described without my having to relay the details to her.

She knew where we were going.

Another nod, her arm stiffening through mine.

For whatever reason, her confirmation of having walked these halls before infuriated me more, my blood warming with the need to punish. To maim. To kill. At some point in the last two weeks, Amara had become mine. And these jackasses had hurt her. More than once.

That, of course, meant her need for vengeance trumped mine, but for the first time in my life, I wanted to assassinate someone out of pure *need*.

All the others were just jobs. Names on a roster

tied to some bad deed or another. I took them out because Arthur requested it.

Franklin and Hampton would die because I *wanted* it.

Amara would deliver the final blow, but I'd guide her. And together we would bathe in their blood.

The thought stirred something inside me, a dark yearning, one tied to the female at my side and the opportunities that existed between us.

This could be my future.

Taking on assignments with this female as my partner.

Oh, Arthur would never allow it.

But maybe it was time to break a few rules. I'd done everything he ever asked of me for longer than I cared to remember, very rarely taking things for myself. The Tabella Della Morte was my first love and my primary mission. But life constantly evolved, and maybe, for once, I wanted something more.

Maybe I wanted Amara. Indefinitely.

An insane notion after so little time, but we clicked. And as my father always told me, sometimes you just know.

No. This is too much.

I shook the thoughts away, refusing to focus on any of it right now. Distractions ruined plans, and I had no intention of fucking this up tonight. It was an in-and-out job. No emotions allowed.

Amara had gone cold beside me, her arm ice against mine.

"Harness it," I whispered, sensing the pain radiating off her. "Use it."

She said nothing, her body seeming to move on autopilot. When we reached the final door, I tried to give her a moment to regroup her thoughts, but she was already turning the handle and stepping inside a typical sitting room.

I glanced around for any perceived threats or security. Nothing out of the ordinary. But Amara kept walking, going directly to a closet.

No, not a closet.

A door to another room.

One that had my stomach churning.

This was the master's playroom, a dungeon of sorts that would typically appeal to my assassin senses. But it provided me with too vivid an insight into the types of things these men had done to her.

Especially as she settled in the middle of the cement floor, on her knees, head bowed.

"Amara?" I whispered, again glancing around and thankfully finding us alone. "What are you doing?"

But it was as if she'd stopped hearing me, her training having taken over in some fucked-up manner.

When I touched her shoulder, I found it ice cold and stiff. She didn't acknowledge me, just took a steadying breath, her hands clasped around the purse on her thighs as she waited.

This was not what we discussed.

I needed her to play a mute sex kitten, to stick the men with the needles when they were too distracted by her body to notice, then force the poison down their throats.

But the Amara before me was a broken doll, a woman retreating into the recesses of her mind and refusing to face reality.

This was the headspace she must fall into when afraid. Or perhaps the state she adopted when she needed to turn off her mind, to accept the pain about to be inflicted on her body.

Fuck.

KILLIAN

I knelt before Amara, needing her to snap out of this as soon as possible. Because Hampton hadn't described this location to me, just the seating area. This was no doubt where he planned to move the party, but we shouldn't know it exists yet.

That he left it unlocked spoke volumes about the unvisited nature of this part of the home. Especially to keep it open during a party. Ballsy as hell. And totally irrelevant.

"Amara," I whispered again, trying to catch her gaze.

No reply, her eyes affixed to the ground as her head remained bowed.

I cupped her cheek to tilt her face upward and took in her vacant expression. She didn't blink, her pupils so dilated I couldn't discern the color of her irises.

"Kitten." I swept my thumb over her bottom lip, which parted on autopilot. She'd been fine only moments ago, but something about the hallway had triggered this reaction. Perhaps a nightmare of sorts, her conditioning kicking in, something that regressed her to this heartbreaking state of a woman trained to be used.

"Starting without us?" Franklin drawled from the doorway, a glass of bourbon in his hand.

Amara's eyes closed, but not before I caught the tear lurking in the corner.

Right.

Plan B.

I pressed a kiss to her forehead, then brushed my lips against her ear. "Don't disappear on me, sweetheart. I'll fix this."

"Making yourself right at home, I see," Hampton said as he joined Franklin.

"I am," I admitted, standing. "Your accommodations are impressive. Although, I was surprised to find the door to your play area unlocked. Were you already expecting someone for the evening?"

"We were shopping," Franklin admitted.

I slowly removed my jacket, not wanting to soil it, and slid it over Amara's shoulders to help shield her from their hungry gazes. "Are there others in attendance selling women?" I wondered, rolling my sleeves while they watched.

"What was it you said?" Hampton glanced sideways as if trying to recall my exact words. "Everything has a price? Right?" He smiled, his gaze falling to the back of Amara's head. "You have her well trained."

I gave him a noncommittal shrug in reply, already tired of this exchange. Just needed to finish protecting my clothes, then we could begin.

"Why is she covered? Is she teasing?" Franklin asked, the yearning in his tone making me want to kill him first.

"I thought you wanted to unwrap her?" I replied, done with my sleeves. I slid my hands into the pockets of my pants to palm a pair of throwing blades.

He sauntered forward, his bourbon in his hand. "I want a closer look at our prize. Let's remove the jacket."

"Sure. You're welcome to try." I didn't step aside, nor did I bend to do his bidding.

"Try?" he repeated, smirking. "Oh, I'll more than try."

Hampton didn't seem as sure, his stance in the doorway holding a touch of uncertainty. Recognition flared in his features as he studied Amara's hair. "Where did you acquire her?" he asked, his hand sliding into his pocket.

"Where did we meet, kitten?" I asked, knowing she wouldn't answer. "Oh, right, Amsterdam." The knife left my palm with a flick of my wrist, nailing Hampton in the torso before he could finish withdrawing whatever item he desired. Franklin's proximity to Amara put him close enough for me to punch him in the face with my blade-throwing hand, sending him flying backward.

I stepped around Amara, the knife from my other palm switching to my favored hand.

Hampton scrambled backward into the adjoining room, my dagger in his abdomen a nuisance more than a disabling throw. Oh, it'd kill him if he didn't seek medical help, but he could still move. As he was doing now.

"What the fuck?" Franklin bellowed.

"You're not of use to me," I said, deciding to end him first. "In fact, you're a fucking irritation." He tried to sit up and shift away from me, but I was fast and practiced, while his athletic form seemed only used to a morning jog at best.

The razor edge of my throwing blade sliced across his throat with ease, crimson fluid bubbling from the wound as he fought to inhale.

"Drowning in your own blood is too easy a death, but we're on a time limit." He clutched his neck, his eyes bulging out of his head, soundless gurgles slipping past his lips.

I ignored him in favor of the bastard fleeing across the floor in the room. He already had a phone in his hand, dialing someone. That must have been the object he had gone for in his pocket. Too bad. I was spoiling for a fight, and it seemed he wouldn't be the one to give it to me.

"Malcom," he spit out as I joined him in the seating area. Fortunately, the door leading to the hallway was closed and appeared to be locked. "Amara's here with a psychopath."

I continued toward him as he backed up into the

couch, his opposite hand against the blade still lodged in his stomach. If he pulled it out, he'd be in even more pain, something he must have known because he didn't try to remove it.

"Tell Jenkins that Killian sends his regards," I said, smiling. "And that I hope he's enjoying his tour around Europe." It hadn't been part of the plan to let him know I was here until he heard about the deaths of his friends. Alas, some situations required improvisation.

"What the fuck is going on?" Hampton demanded, flinching at the blade in his abdomen.

"You're a monster who rapes and abuses women. And I'm here to ensure you never procreate," I summarized. "Oh, and you have your buddy Jenkins to thank for all of this."

He held up a bloody hand as I stepped closer. "Wait. We can work this out. I have money, friends in high places, anything you need." He held out the phone. "Whatever your beef with Malcom is, I want no part of it. You can have him."

"I assure you that you have absolutely nothing I want or need, and begging only makes you look weak. But I'll accept this, thank you." I took the phone. "Do you hear that, Malcom? It's the sound of your empire collapsing around you."

"Mister Bedivere," Malcom replied, as calm and collected as ever. "Surely there is some sort of arrangement we can come to. This is just exhausting, isn't it?"

"Exhausting?" I repeated with a humorless laugh. "No, Senator. It's exhilarating." To prove my point, I knelt and ran my blade across Hampton's throat the same way I did Franklin's. His shriek died in a series of gurgles I made sure Malcom heard through the phone. "Sorry, I assume you alerted the authorities while trying to stall me, and didn't feel I had time to delay."

His responding silence confirmed my suspicion.

"Well, it's been great catching up with you, but I really must be going. Don't worry, though. I'll see you soon. And Assad, too." I pressed End and slid the phone into my pocket.

Hampton stared up at me with glassy eyes, his death imminent.

"You deserved worse," I said, frustrated that he'd died so easily.

I turned to find Amara observing from the doorway, my jacket still around her shoulders, her fingers white against her clutch. "I... I..." She visibly shook, her lips trembling.

I had her in my arms several steps later, pulling her against me in a hug while doing my best not to touch her with the bloody dagger. "It's okay, sweetheart."

We really didn't have time to waste, not with the police on their way, but I couldn't just drag her out of here. Not in her current state.

She collapsed into me, her body trembling violently against mine as incomprehensible words left her mouth. Something about losing herself, fear, and a word I despised—failure.

"You didn't fail," I promised her. "You're incredibly resilient to even be standing in this room. That's not a failure, Amara. It's a sign of strength." I checked my watch, flinching. "Kitten, I need you to call on that part of you, the fighter in you, the one that allowed you to walk into the ballroom tonight with unrestrained confidence. Because we need to go."

There was no time for cleanup. No time to hide our presence here. Running was our only option.

Thankfully, we'd been in masks the entire time.

Unfortunately, Amara's prints would be all over this room. And likely the prints of countless other women. Maybe even men, too. I touched nothing other than her, my blades, and Hampton's phone. All items I would be taking with us.

"Wh-what?" she mumbled, pulling back to study me, her gaze red from crying.

"The police are coming," I whispered. And while I'd dealt with those types of issues before, her presence would make that task much more difficult. "Can you try to walk with me?"

"I… I… Yes." She swallowed, her eyes seeming to clear as she shook her head. "Yes, of course."

I glanced around, searching for any further evidence of our presence here. Amara still had her clothes, shoes, purse, my jacket. I returned to Hampton, wiping the blood off on his jacket as best I could before retrieving my other throwing dagger and repeating the process. Then I slid them into my pocket beside his phone and reached for Amara's hand. She grabbed it like a lifeline, her pale cheeks making me concerned that she might relapse again.

I tugged her toward the door, then released her to grab the sleeve of my jacket hanging from her arm. Using it as a glove, I unlocked and twisted the knob, then peeked out into the hallway.

Silence.

Chances were the police were near the front gates, which would be blocked by all the cars waiting for their owners outside.

Thank fuck for well-attended masquerade balls.

"Let's go," I said, leading her into the corridor and using my makeshift glove to close the door. Releasing my jacket, I found her hand again and began a swift walk back toward the party with her keeping up at my side.

She said nothing.

I said nothing.

Until we reached the main hall, where it was abuzz with energy.

The cops had definitely arrived.

Thinking quickly, I pulled her into an alcove near the side and clasped her hands between my palms. "Do you trust me?" I asked, my gaze burning into hers.

Her eyes answered me before her mouth did. "I

do."

"Good. I need to kiss you. Someone will interrupt us soon; pretend to be drunk and dazed." I wrapped my palm around the back of her neck, holding her where I wanted her. "Okay?"

She nodded quickly, her hurried exhale feathering over my lips.

This was the last thing I should be doing after her episode in the other room, but it was our best chance at an alibi.

I took her mouth with mine, careful not to unleash all my pent-up frustration and aggression onto her. Gentle and tender were enough to trick an onlooker. Especially with Amara in this stunning dress.

She returned the embrace, her lips tentative beneath mine, her hands curling into my sides. It wasn't so much awkward as it was sweet, something I didn't usually do but was what she needed. After everything she'd endured, Amara deserved someone who could be kind to her, cherish her, give her a normal life.

A man who definitely wasn't me.

I preferred violence, blood, revenge. I thrived on chaos. I enjoyed hurting others, like Hampton and

Franklin.

Delivering punishments was my livelihood.

Amara required a future away from this world. Away from me.

She bit my lower lip, hard, causing my eyes to lift to hers. The warrior I adored glowered up at me. "Kiss. Me."

"I am."

She shook her head, her nails digging into my side, her pupils narrowing even more. "It's not the same."

Yeah, because I didn't want to hurt her. Obviously. "Amara—"

"I *need* you to touch me." The plea in her voice startled me. "Please, Killian. I'm not broken. I don't want pity. I... I need you to prove that I'm not... *Please*. I don't..." She trailed off, her lips lifting to mine. Tentative. Soft. Imploring.

I opened my mouth to receive her tongue, allowing her to take charge in my confusion. She thought I pitied her? That I considered her broken?

No.

She was one of the strongest women I'd ever met, her will to survive a heady presence I longed to be closer to. Amara continued to floor me, her reactions nothing like I anticipated, always throwing me off my game.

Just like she did now as she demanded my reciprocation, her teeth chastising me with bites along my lip for not giving her what she wanted. Her body arched into mine, my jacket falling from her shoulders to the floor as she wrapped her arms around my neck and tugged me down to her. Claiming me. Owning me. Possessing me.

What started as a need for an alibi blossomed into so much more.

Amara was hurting.

And she required my brand of healing.

Fuck tender.

She wanted passion.

Pain mingled with pleasure.

A reminder of how to feel *good*.

I tangled my fingers in her hair, not caring at all that she'd styled it for the evening, and tugged her head back to a better angle. And let myself go, giving her what she requested and swallowing her responding whimper.

Yes.

She'd been hurt. She'd fallen into the past. But it was on me to bring her back to the present, to show her the future.

All those misleading thoughts about what she required were wrong.

I was the one she needed.

Right now.

Right here.

I kissed her harder, her moans urging me onward. Pressing her into the wall of the alcove, I gave her everything she begged for and more. Her nails ran up my sides, then down to my hips, her fingers undoing my belt with experienced ease.

I should stop her, some part of me thought. An angelic side. A good side.

But the darker part of me overrode my common sense and encouraged her to continue. That part of me was tied to my throbbing dick.

"Killian," she breathed, arching into me. Keeping one hand in her hair, I slid the other to her hip. Her dress had slits up both sides to her mid-thighs, providing easy access to the flesh beneath.

"Tell me what you want," I whispered, no longer caring about repercussions or the chaos going on in the hallway beyond us. Amara was all I could think of, all I could see.

"You," she said, her fingers drawing down my zipper. "In me."

Fuck, this couldn't be more wrong.

Here, of all places.

Now, after everything that had happened.

Except, I was helpless to stop her, especially as she palmed me through my boxer briefs.

Amara needed me.

Her fingers freed my cock, wrapping around it and giving me an alluring stroke. "Please, Killian," she said on a groan. "Fuck me. Bring me back to you. Remind me where I am, *who* I am."

This woman was going to get me killed.

Oh, but I'd die a happy man.

She dropped to her knees, taking me into her mouth and sucking me hard. I cursed, my arm going to the wall to keep me from falling. "Amara…" My opposite hand remained in her hair, urging her to continue.

It made me a horrible person.

A knight with a black streak a mile long.

And fuck if I cared, not with her pretty lips wrapped around my shaft, her throat working as she hollowed her cheeks.

Damn, she was amazing.

But I wanted to be inside her. To feel her cunt squeeze me as I fucked her hard, long, and deep.

I yanked her upward, eliciting a groan of protest from her that I swallowed with my mouth. Her dress bunched around her hips, my hands working before I could even protest the motion.

And damn, she wasn't wearing any panties.

I could seriously love this woman.

"Legs around my waist, kitten," I demanded, lifting her.

She greeted my cock with a wet kiss from between her thighs, her body arching into mine to accept me on my first thrust. My forehead fell to hers, the heaven of her welcome nearly causing me to come right then and there. But I needed her to join me in this sweet oblivion, to take me over the edge by coming around me.

"This is going to be hard and fast," I warned.

"Good." She drove me deeper with a flex of her hips, her nails in my hair as she took my mouth with an animalistic force. I gave in to the impulses surrounding us, taking her the way I craved in a manner she openly received.

Each push forward elicited a quiver from her, a new scratch on my scalp, a bite against my lips. She'd worked herself into a frenzy, one I tried to temper but found myself falling headfirst into reciprocating.

Killing always stirred up an adrenaline high, and she feasted on it now, coaxing it to pour out of me in waves as I fucked her up against the wall. If the authorities interrupted us now, I'd kill them on principle alone. My woman required release, and I was going to give it to her regardless of our audience.

She panted against me, her heart thrumming wildly in time with mine, as we stroked the combustible energy building between us.

"More," she whimpered, blood trickling down my lip from where she'd bitten me. "More, Killian."

I knew better than to pull out my blades, so I used my hands. Balancing her against the wall with my hips alone, I palmed her breasts through the thin fabric and pinched her stiff peaks. Not nicely. But harshly. And she practically sang against my mouth, her approval evident in the way she shuddered.

Her need for pain fueled my desires more, bringing me that much closer to coming.

The urgency increased our pace. She nipped at me again, her teeth dragging across my jaw to my earlobe. I twisted her nipple before she could bite me, earning me a delicious moan from the base of her throat. My name followed on a growl as she came apart against me, her slick walls clamping down on my cock.

"*Fuck.*" I grabbed her hair again, forcing her lips to mine as I found my own release inside her. Agony mingled with rapture, causing my legs to shake as I emptied everything I possessed into her tight little body. And she took it all, accepting every part of me while kissing me with a vengeance. Every time with her was more intense than the last, and this was no different.

I shook against her, my chest heaving from the exertion, and still she demanded more from my mouth. She seemed starved for my tongue, for me.

But with the edge taken off, I knew this couldn't continue. We'd be found any second now. At least our alibi would check out.

"Amara, sweetheart," I whispered, bringing her back down.

She shook her head, refusing to leave our blissful cloud, her nails embedded in the back of my neck. I eased myself out of her slowly, confused for a moment at the new sensation until I realized that, in my rush to take her, I'd forgotten a condom.

Damn.

That was a first.

Hell, this entire night was a first.

I brought a date with me to an assassination.

I messed up the kill by becoming distracted by her emotional state.

And now I'd fucked her up against a wall instead of focusing on the commotion in the hallway.

We needed to get the hell out of here before I did something else, like confess to the cops and find myself in a jail cell.

I forced her to stand while I zipped myself up, deciding the sloppy look between us would actually aid in our escape.

It'd be very obvious what we were doing in this little nook. And if I played it right, they'd assume it was a drunken encounter. I messed up my hair to add to the look, loosened my tie, and haphazardly tightened my belt. Then I took in Amara's delicious state with her dress still hiked up over her hips, her auburn strands tousled to seductive perfection. She gave me a drowsy look through her mask, her blue-green eyes smiling.

"You enjoyed that," I murmured.

"I want more," she countered.

"Yeah?" I cupped her freshly fucked pussy, feeling my cum mingle with her juices on my fingers, then lifted them to her mouth. "Suck them clean for me."

Her lips parted, her tongue gliding over my skin as she did exactly as I requested without breaking eye contact.

My Amara was back—the wanton warrior with a confident streak few others possessed.

And damn, was I happy to see her.

She released my final finger with a pop. "Thank you, sir." Her chosen nickname for me went straight to my balls, causing me to want to fuck her all over again.

But reason won in the end, my hands working to fix her dress and giving her a more presentable appearance.

Her pleasure-drunk stare worked in my favor, her swollen lips leaving no questions as to what we'd been doing.

Screw being found.

One look at the pair of us and we'd be excused.

I bent to pick up my jacket, returning it to her shoulders, and slid her clutch into the interior pocket so no one would think to search it.

"Let's get you home." Not to Powell's estate, but to one of my safe houses. Because Malcom and Assad would be on their way back from Europe now, and I had no intention of making it easy for them to find us.

"Okay," she agreed, the smile in her voice putting my heart at ease in a way I couldn't explain.

I did that.

I fixed her.

She didn't need normal.

She needed me.

And I rather liked that revelation.

I allowed it to show on my lips and in my eyes as I tugged her into view of everyone in the corridor, her arm looped through mine as we stumbled across the marble, high from our explosive sex. The knives were still in my pockets. The poison and ketamine in the purse hidden beneath my suit jacket.

But no one thought to question us, a glance at our appearance causing the cops to look right through us, their displeasure at our behavior evident. If they only knew.

We danced around the onlookers, most of whom had removed their masks in confusion, and pretended not to notice all the men in uniform. One or two of them tried to ask us questions, but my incoherent answers left us quickly dismissed.

All in all, a close call, but a successful evening.

And enlightening, too.

Amara wasn't ready to face her enemies yet. I could remove them all on my own, but it wouldn't provide her with the closure she required.

However, I had a plan. One Arthur wasn't going to care for, but he didn't get a say in this mission. Not anymore.

This was between me and Amara.

And those who had wronged her.

We would kill them all—together—when my partner was ready.

AMARA

Five Weeks Later...

"Consider it this way, Arthur. I'm giving you time to find higher bidders." Killian's voice lured me to the living area, where he sat on the couch, admiring the waves crashing outside on the beach below.

We'd spent a little over a month here, training on the shores of Virginia where he swore no one would ever find us. With spring coming, there were a few tourists popping around, but it was otherwise quiet.

For the first week, I kept glancing over my shoulder expecting Malcom to be waiting for me, but apparently, not even Killian's closest friends knew about this home. It was his secret place, the one he ran to when he wanted to avoid everyone and the world.

The circumstance may have required this invite

to his secret hideout, but he didn't seem to mind my presence. If anything, he seemed to be enjoying it.

"I know," he said into the phone. He held out his arm for me to join him on the couch, his constant awareness warming my blood. Killian always knew when I was near, even when I approached quietly from behind—like now.

I settled beside him on the sofa, my head falling to his shoulder as he snorted. "A decade of concise assassinations earns me a brief vacation, Calthorpe. Besides, I'm about to make you a fortune when I finish taking out this list."

His boss's deep voice was too low for me to hear his response.

"Yes, I'm aware of the whispers," Killian replied. "If I decide to move on them, you'll be the first to know."

More words that I couldn't comprehend.

"I know how to do my fucking job. I'll complete it when I'm ready." He fell quiet as the other man spoke. "I appreciate that. Yes." He laughed then, the sound harsh. "You're right; I don't care."

A short murmur followed, then Killian set down

the phone. Arthur must have hung up without a goodbye or something. "Is he mad?" I wondered, not wanting to piss off the man Killian considered his boss.

"Arthur doesn't get mad. That would imply he has emotions." He leaned his head back and blew out a sigh. "But yes, he wants me to wrap up this job. On the plus side, I officially have the go-ahead to add Clarissa and Geoff Rose to our list. Of course, we were going to kill them anyway, but now at least he'll profit from it."

"When?" I asked.

He'd put all our plans on hold after the incident in Charlotte. At first, I'd argued with him, saying it was just a minor setback, and accused him of babying me. But after some reflection, I realized he was right to pause our efforts.

I'd frozen at the Hampton estate, my memories assaulting me from all angles and forcing me into a "safe" mindset. Killian had pulled me out of it by killing Franklin. But it'd still taken me several minutes to process what had happened. It seemed natural for me to hide, to disappear into the recesses of my mind and block out the pain associated with that horrid place.

I didn't regret the regression, had accepted it as a setback and a learning experience. One I intended to learn from to push forward.

Killian was a patient teacher, mostly, but harsh when I needed him to be. Beneath his instruction, I almost felt ready to face anything.

Almost.

"Soon," he replied, reaching over to squeeze my knee. He was just as eager to take everyone down as I was, but he also knew I had to be in the right mind frame to help him. Rather than take it all on by himself, he was waiting. Something I sensed was new to him, just like everything else between us.

Hmm, although, I'd come to know him well these last two months, which was how I caught the tick in his jaw. It meant Arthur had said something that unsettled him, something he continued to think about.

"What whispers did Arthur mention?" I asked, wondering if that was what had him perplexed.

Killian exhaled softly—confirming my suspicion—while his thumb traced a pattern against the bare skin beneath my jean shorts. "Another auction," he finally admitted. "Arthur picked it up on his channels, as did Raven."

I considered the timeline.

Killian had mentioned there was one shortly after the masquerade. I'd been livid when he refused to go. Now I recognized that it'd been for the best.

Demons lurked inside me, creating a darkness that needed to be exorcised in healthy ways—such as in the bedroom with Killian. And I harbored a deep-seated need for revenge, one that clawed at my heart, begging to be released. However, it had to be under the right set of circumstances. Not rushed. Or I'd freeze again, just like I did in Jefferson's playroom.

But now I knew how it felt, the signs of an episode coming on, and with Killian's help, I was learning how to dispel my innate reactions to it. To trust in myself to see beyond the past and focus on the future.

The terrors would never leave me; they were what gave me a reason to fight, what bolstered my tough spirit today. Using those nightmares made me stronger. My experiences were weapons, all contrived to help me seek revenge. Killian helped me sharpen those weapons, molding them into deadly tools I could wield in a fight.

Instead of hiding

"They usually host one auction a month," I finally said, responding to his comment about my former captors. "So the timeline marries up to what I know about them."

He nodded, his gaze taking on a faraway gleam, one that radiated a fury I felt to the depths of my soul.

"You want to go after them now." I recognized the hard glimmer in his pupils, knew it radiated in my own. "When is it scheduled to take place?"

"Next weekend," he replied, his arm tensing across my shoulders. "But as you said, there will always be another. And another. We can take our time and plan this."

"While more innocent lives are traded for money." I shook my head. "You know I can't let that slide." This was different from the last time we had this conversation. My head and heart were in the right place now, in agreement for how we needed to proceed. "I feel almost ready, Killian."

"*Almost* isn't good enough."

"But we have another week. Maybe by then..." I trailed off on a shrug. "You're the one who always wants to plan. So let's develop a two-tiered strategy, the first one being on the chance that I'm truly ready, and the second being a backup scenario in case I'm not. It doesn't hurt to practice, right?" I prodded his side, knowing he'd appreciate my turn of words.

He glanced at me sideways. "It's like you actually listen to me when I talk, kitten."

My lips curled. "Well, you once told me talking is foreplay, so consider me always engaged when you speak."

He chuckled and pulled me into his lap to nuzzle my nose with his own, the action one that bespoke of a comfort new to both of us. Killian confided in me that he didn't usually date, a consequence of his job. But things between us were different.

I knew everything about him even though I shouldn't. Just as he understood me in a way no one else ever had.

It placed us in this stasis of comfort where we just existed, never questioning the intention or future, just embracing the moment and taking it one day at a time.

I liked it here. Felt happy here. Wanted to remain here.

But I meant what I said—I couldn't just stand by and allow more innocent lives to be corrupted by Geoff and Clarissa Rose. Not when I finally had the means to take them down.

I owed it to those who would come after me, to end this.

Hell, I owed it to myself to seek vengeance.

And I would, when the time was right. Which, instinct told me, was now.

I could only reside in my utopia bubble with Killian for so long. Eventually, we had to leave, to move on, to face the monsters who haunted my past. And finish them once and for all.

Killian held my gaze, an unspoken agreement passing between us. He sighed, nodding. "Two plans. We only proceed if we both agree you're ready."

I studied him, knowing he would never hold me back for his own personal gain. He would let me fly when he believed it was time because Killian didn't believe in grounding others. He helped them grow, to survive on their own.

Killian Bedivere claimed not to be a hero.

However, I saw the truth. I saw *him*, my lethal knight who emboldened and enlightened me. The one who instructed me on how to use my inner spirit effectively and efficiently, to fight. The assassin who trusted me enough with his own secrets to provide me with a glimpse into his dangerous world, and protect me from it at the same time.

This man may claim not to be a good guy, and maybe he wasn't by traditional standards, but he was by my definition. And I adored him all the more for it.

"We only proceed if we both agree I'm ready," I agreed, parroting his words back at him. Killian had done everything in his power to strengthen me over the last two months. He wouldn't stop now by smothering my growth. I trusted his opinion, just as he trusted mine.

He grabbed my hips. "Then I suggest we go outside and spar on the beach."

"You just want to get me naked again." It happened every time we fought. His skills far surpassed mine, though he claimed I had a natural speed that made him work for it. Still, he ended up on top of me every damn time. And I always lost my clothes in the process.

"Of course." He nibbled my jaw. "It's my sole motivation for teaching you to fight, Amara. You know how I love putting my hands on you."

"Uh-huh." I put my hands on his chest. "Except it's usually your knives doing all the touching."

"To remove the clothes in the way of my hands," he explained, grinning.

I raised a brow. "Then explain the scratch marks on my breasts."

"A moment of excitement."

"And my inner thighs?" Which tingled just at the thought of the tiny nicks he'd left there last night before going down on me for well over an hour.

"Teasing," he murmured, not at all apologetic. Not that he needed to be. We both knew I enjoyed it.

Still... "One of these days, I'll use a blade on you and see how you like it."

"Oh, Amara." He threaded his fingers through my hair, tightening his hold and pressing his lips to mine. "That would require you to best me."

"I will," I promised against his mouth.

"Maybe," he whispered, kissing me softly. "Now stop distracting me. We have work to do outside."

"Yes, sir," I teased, mostly because I knew he enjoyed it. And also because the nickname seemed to fit him.

Sir Bedivere.

My dark knight.

My version of a hero.

My... *love.*

AMARA

I touched the black feathered mask hiding my cheekbones and forehead, barely recognizing myself in the floor-to-ceiling mirror. The woman staring back at me resembled a stranger with her freshly dyed black hair and brown contacts. But I recognized the body beneath the formfitting gown as mine, just as I knew the man beside me.

Killian wore an ebony suit, no tie, and a matching mask. It covered more of his face than the one he wore to the masquerade gala, the requirements for tonight's event being more about concealing one's identity than having fun in the name of charity.

Something told me Jefferson's choice of gala theme had been a throwback to his preferred circle of deviance—the one surrounding us now.

Killian's palm burned against my lower back, the

cut of my dress leaving my entire spine exposed. It was par for the course in this crowd—the more seductively elegant, the better. And we needed to blend in.

He guided us past the mirror-lined entryway into one of the many living areas inside Clarissa and Geoff's estate. This was the Massachusetts residence I grew up in, the one that provided an opulent appearance on the upper levels and a dungeon beneath.

I'd provided Killian with a detailed layout of the property, and also expectations for tonight. Then his hacker friend had worked some magic to get us on the invite list.

Tonight we were known as Mr. and Mrs. Daggerington—a recently wed couple, with Killian being in business mergers and acquisitions. Raven manufactured a background that included a few details about our darker bedroom behaviors to suggest our purpose here. Just enough to provide Clarissa with the blackmail she required to grant us entry. Because that was what she cared about most—her ability to control the products on display and the clients purchasing them. It was how she safeguarded her lucrative business.

Which meant everyone in this room was a deviant.

Not that I needed to know that detail to determine their natures. It was written in the way they interacted with tonight's auction items.

Most of the girls had guards who helped maintain a strict "look, but don't touch" policy.

The remaining women weren't as fortunate. They resembled the used-and-returned goods and were up for purchase again. Which meant they could be borrowed and played with by the consumers in the room as a sort of sick and twisted trial run before tonight's auction began.

And several were taking advantage of the testing period right now.

Girls were surrounded, being forced to perform unspeakable sexual acts that made my stomach churn.

That used to be me.

Although, not nearly as wretched. I was passed around a few parties like this, but Clarissa always required me to remain clothed. Albeit scandalously, but it kept the men from sticking things inside me. Like their cocks.

I shivered. Too many memories of my previous life hung in this place. I wanted to burn it to the ground, destroy it all.

To never hear any of those screams again, or the gagging...

Fuck.

A heavy sense of foreboding hit me, a reminder that this could have become my future under Malcom's harsh rule. His private affairs were usually smaller, with no more than a few friends, but had he ever tired of me, this was what I'd have been returned to.

Killian's lips brushed my pulse, ever aware of my reactions and thoughts. "You okay, kitten?" he asked against my ear.

I nodded. While I felt ill, I was still controlling it.

The last two months with him had taught me so much about myself. I'd always been a fighter with a strong will to survive. However, Killian helped me learn how to sharpen that will into a lethal weapon, one I intended to use tonight.

I turned to look up at him, running my fingers over his cheek and down his neck, my signal to him that I could handle this. That I *was* handling it. He angled his head to nip the pad of my index finger, his lips curling.

Despite all the sounds of sick depravity shadowing this room, that smile had my heart skipping a beat in anticipation. Tonight, I would have my vengeance.

I lifted onto my toes—my four-inch stilettos not giving me enough height—and pressed my mouth to his. To an onlooker, it would appear I was aroused by the sights of the room. But Killian would understand my true intent.

Thank you for being here.

I can do this.

Trust me.

You're my salvation.

His tongue whispered responses across my lips, inside my mouth, grounding me with each stroke. The nightmares of my past may be present here, but I no longer lived in those moments.

I escaped on my own, had gone toe-to-toe with this assassin and won our first dance, then gave in to him after our second. And I'd not regretted any of it. He completed me in a way I never knew I needed, coaxing my warrior side to better herself and fight instead of run.

Now it was time for my warrior soul to play and

to bask in the blood of her enemies.

I nibbled his lower lip, smiling. "I'm ready."

"I know," he murmured. "Where's your target?"

He meant Clarissa.

Geoff would be handled after her.

"Upstairs," I said without bothering to look around.

Killian had wanted to see how many people we were dealing with, which was the only reason we'd started in the living area. There were maybe forty patrons and six or seven auction items. Pretty standard attendance. Everyone wore masks to protect their identities, not that it mattered. They were all too far gone in their own depravities to care about anyone else, including our unexpected arrival. Of course, they all relied on the estate security to discern who could enter and who couldn't.

Upstairs would be different.

Everyone would notice us there.

"Seems rude for the hostess to leave a party unattended." He kept his voice low for my ears alone. Although, everyone else was too consumed with their activities to pay attention to us, anyway.

"She provides specialized demos for her most valuable clients." I'd been a demonstration on more than one occasion, so I knew the procedure well. The only difference between me and the others was that no one had been allowed to fuck me. Touching, yes. Penetration, no.

Killian's mouth touched mine, bringing me back to him again. "Shame we didn't make the list."

"We could always crash the party, make our presence known?"

"I adore that idea, kitten," he replied. "As I imagine you won't mind if a few of her precious clients are caught up in the mess along the way?"

"Oh, I'm counting on that." Killian had brought more than knives to this party, and I very much wanted to see him in action. "But there will be a few innocents up there."

"I have good aim," he promised, kissing me again. "Lead the way."

Taking his hand, I pulled him toward the back of the living area and into a corridor that led to one of the dining rooms. Beyond it was a kitchen meant for manor staff only. Given the majority were on the floor serving drinks and hors d'oeuvres, it left only a few meandering around in the background.

They were all servants of the illegal variety, not paid employees. Which meant they were all victims who had somehow survived the horrors of their lives, only to end up working in a kitchen serving the two demons who had ruined them to begin with.

It was a horrible cycle, one that needed to end.

They were too broken to care about our presence, barely even raising their heads to acknowledge us. So it wasn't a surprise when none of them questioned us as I opened the door to the back stairs—the ones only the manor staff used.

Killian stepped along behind me, the space too narrow for us to walk up side by side. He caught my wrist as we reached the top—a door hiding the hallway beyond it from our view.

I glanced back to see him staring down at his phone with a frown.

"What is it?" I asked, whispering.

"A really weird text." He showed me the screen.

K - I have to tell you about my date from last night. That frat guy, remember? Steve? Anyway, remind me to give you the deets later. Talk about a total douche canoe! Really, really bad. Almost unreal, dude. Please call me when you have a min. -R Bird.

"R Bird?" I repeated, my brow furrowing. Then my eyebrows lifted. "Raven."

"Yeah, but I don't know what the fuck she's trying to tell me." He started to reply when his jaw tightened. "Oh. Oh, fuck." I watched as he pulled the first letter of each sentence into a new message.

K - I. T. S. A. T. R. A. P. - R

I didn't know how he caught that so quickly, but imagined it went with the territory of his job. He grabbed my hand and pulled me back down the stairs toward the kitchen, his movements sharp and precise.

But a familiar face stood waiting for us at the bottom.

One that made my blood run cold.

Killian stood before me as if protecting me from the sight of my former "fiancé." But the sound of heels on the stairs behind us had me turning to see another nightmare come to life.

Clarissa pointed a gun at my head, her aim very likely to be true at this close range. Unfortunately, she was smart enough not to move within grabbing range. Killian had taught me a few ways to disarm someone, none of which would help me at this angle.

Shit!

Taviv appeared beside Malcom, nudging him to the side and aiming a weapon at Killian. "Weapons. Now." The authority in the male's tone scattered goose bumps across my skin.

"Or she dies," Clarissa added, as if it wasn't clear by the barrel aimed at my skull.

"All right. Everything is in my jacket," Killian said, removing his hands from his pockets slowly and opening them to show he held nothing. He slid the wool from his shoulders and tossed the clothing downward, where it landed at Taviv's feet with a thud.

There go our guns.

"Shoes," Taviv demanded next.

Killian kicked off his shoes, sending them down the stairs. Then bent to show off his socks. "Nothing there."

"Walk down here. Slowly. Amara stays."

Killian shrugged, completely at ease. How he managed to feel fine about all this floored me. Did he have a secondary plan we hadn't discussed? Because none of our ideas involved being surprised by Malcom and Taviv.

Which meant Amir lurked nearby.

My stomach twisted in the worst way, my mouth going dry, my hands beginning to shake.

And Killian left me on the stairs, his steps slow and even as he descended toward Taviv.

What if he shoots Killian? He's my only hope at escape!

Sweat trickled across my brow despite the ice swimming through my veins. This wasn't supposed to happen. Clarissa and Geoff were supposed to be here with a bunch of sex-possessed monsters, stewing in a world of violence that we intended to make even bloodier.

Not this.

Not Killian walking toward Taviv with his hands raised.

He had to have some sort of idea to get us out of this.

As he hit the last stair, Malcom's fist met Killian's face, sending him backward into the wall. Rather than fight back, he merely looked at him. "I see why you went into politics, Senator. You wouldn't survive a day in my world throwing punches like that."

Taviv hit him next, the butt of his gun slamming into Killian's skull and sending him to the floor with a grunt.

He didn't move.

Knocked out.

Oh God… This is really happening.

Because Killian wasn't faking it. He would never stay down like that. Right? Maybe? Fuck, it could—

Taviv kicked him in the side. Apart from his body jolting from the impact, he didn't otherwise react.

Definitely unconscious.

Fuck!

Now what? I couldn't fight them all on my own. I was strong, yes, but they had weapons. I did not.

"Finish him," Clarissa ordered.

"No." The chilling voice came from the top of the stairs, the raspy quality identifying Amir even in the dark. Of course, I always knew him. He had a presence about him, an air of danger, that I felt whenever he was near. And it terrified me. "You do not command my men."

Clarissa's lips pursed. "Fine. Then you tell him to do it." She hadn't stopped pointing the gun at my head. Part of me wanted to lunge for her, preferring death to watching them kill Killian.

"No. I want him alive. For now." Amir finally came into view, his lean form covered in what was likely a ten-thousand-dollar suit. He didn't do cheap or normal, always extravagant and in charge. It was why he and Malcom were suitable partners. "The girl, too."

Clarissa's painted lips flattened, then she sighed as she lowered the gun. "Of course."

My eyebrows threatened to lift, shock coursing through my veins.

Did the infamous Madam just yield to Amir Assad?

She never gave in to anyone, always claiming to be in charge. But perhaps the dominance emanating from him forced her to submit, even as queen of this house.

"Remove your dress, Amara," Amir said, his voice brooking no argument. "We need to know you're unarmed."

Yes, I was sure that was why they wanted me naked.

"Now," he added when I didn't immediately jump to obey him.

"No." The world slipped from my mouth unbidden, my shoulders rigid, my hands unmoving. "No." If he wanted me to undress, he could come down here and make me. It was what he probably desired anyway, though he would be in no way gentle about it.

Clarissa tsked, her expression radiating disgust. "Two months away from home and you forget who you are." Her palm connected with my cheek so fast I barely caught her movement toward me on the stairs.

But it put her within range.

My fist connected with her jaw, sending her backward into the cement stairs behind her. I raised my foot to stab her with the edge of my heel, but a pair of steel arms wrapped around me and lifted me into the air.

Taviv's musky cologne filled my nostrils, his muscles rigid against my back and around my center. *Fuck this.* I kicked backward at his leg, hitting my target on my first try.

And then my head met the wall. Hard.

Everything spun, my ears ringing, and suddenly

Malcom was right in front of me, his expression one that haunted my nightmares. Not angry, no. He didn't allow others to see him in a pissed-off state. Instead he channeled it into darker activities. And those punishments were swimming in his icy gaze.

"It seems you've forgotten all your training, baby," he murmured, brushing the back of his hand down my cheek. "Perhaps we can fuck it back into you, yes?"

Shivers raced up and down my limbs, leaving me cold. Taviv's nearness, the way his body seemed to harden against mine, made me wish for death over what they had in mind.

Killian...

Why would he let them hit him like that? Why not fight? I'd seen him take down armed men before without batting an eye. So why allow them to win now?

He had to have a plan.

Something up his sleeve to save us.

Or maybe he'd known there was no other option, that we'd lost, and he'd accepted his fate.

No. Killian wouldn't just give up. That wasn't in his nature, and it wasn't in mine, either. Not anymore.

No more hiding.

No more whimpering.

No more escaping to that place inside while they violated my body.

Tonight, I would remain in the present and wait for the moment to fight. I would allow their torment to fuel my need for survival, to sharpen my fury into a lethal tool.

I trusted Killian. He always found a way to win, and I wasn't about to let him down now by giving up.

Malcom slapped me hard across the face, his blue eyes simmering. "I asked you a question, slut. Answer me."

I tilted my head to the side, done being his obedient little fuck doll. "Good luck, *Malcom*." He hated when I addressed him by his first name and not *sir*. Well, no longer would I just lie down and take it.

His palm connected with my cheek, sending my head to the side while Taviv kept me standing. "You dare address me as your equal?"

A laugh escaped me, my mind fracturing between the need to obey and the desire to curse him.

I'd never stood up to him. Ever. And it felt oddly liberating now to do so.

Our surroundings, the violence radiating through the stairwell, and the arms holding me captive should be forcing me to heel. But instead it fueled me. It *angered* me. I had escaped once. I would do it again. These assholes could take my body, but they couldn't take my soul. Not unless I allowed it. And I fucking refused.

I spit in his face. "Fuck. You."

He hit me again, causing me to laugh harder.

"You're fucking weak," I told him, blood pooling in my mouth.

He raised his hand to repeat the action, but Amir caught it before his fist could land. "Enough," he said calmly. "She clearly wants to play. So take her downstairs and play, Malcom. Meanwhile, I have a few things to arrange with Clarissa." His stoic gaze swept over me before landing on Taviv. "Put Bedivere in a cell nearby so he can hear her scream."

KILLIAN

Ugh. What is that shrieking noise, and how the hell do I turn it off? I groaned as I rolled to my side, my head aching like a son of a bitch. And that damn yelling was not helping. Neither was the cold, wet concrete beneath me.

Had I fallen asleep in an alley behind a bar? Because I felt fucking hungover. Like I'd just spent a night out with Nikolai drinking too much of his damn vodka.

Potent shit.

Tasted like acid.

But the Russian loved it.

My body did not.

Another scream rent the air, this one familiar and sending a chill down my spine. *Amara?* The masculine laughs that followed had me stilling, memories threatening my throbbing skull.

Lava flowed through my veins, bringing me to life, invigorating my senses. It smelled like urine down here. And sex. Not a pleasant combination, nor was the realization of just where I'd ended up and how.

What time is it?

I had sent a text off to Nikolai the second I translated Raven's warning. We had a pact, a code only he understood. It'd been my last-ditch effort in case something happened to me, because he was the only one I trusted to help Amara. He knew me better than anyone, and while we'd not discussed it at length, he'd caught on to how I felt about her. He'd follow my signal, and rain hell on everyone if he found me dead.

If they destroyed my phone, it wouldn't matter.

Arthur knew where we were tonight.

It wouldn't be too hard for the Cavalieri to track us down, even if we were moved. But something told me we were still in the Rose estate. If they'd knocked me out to transport us somewhere else, then I'd be a hell of a lot groggier.

I would have to repay *Taviv* later for the pistol-whip to the head. Or, at least, I assumed that was the name of the jackass who had knocked me out. He fit

Amara's description and certainly knew how to knock a guy out. Unlike her former fiancé, who could really use some boxing training.

I rolled to my back, searching my surroundings.

Cement walls. Dirty floor. A well-used bed. And bars.

No guard, or any cameras. Just a standard, unkempt cell.

This type of shit didn't happen to me often, mostly because I fought my way out of problems. But this time had been different. It was either take the hit, or fight and risk Amara being harmed in the crossfire. There'd been no real choice. I sacrificed myself for her, something I had originally warned her I would never do.

Alas, here I was. In a dungeon cell. With my ankle shackled to the wall.

Shit.

Taviv, or one of the other assholes, had stripped me, leaving me bare down to my boxers. They'd even taken my damn socks. No wonder I was freezing.

If Nikolai found me like this, he'd laugh his ass off.

As he would hopefully be here soon, I had best start moving.

Beginning with the metal clasped around my ankle.

I studied the contraption, somewhat disappointed in the old material. One would think the Roses could invest in higher-quality dungeon instruments. However, I supposed it probably worked on their standard female prisoner.

But not me.

The thick ring anchoring the chain into the concrete floor looked pretty sturdy, and it was wide enough to thread the rusty metal through it.

Yeah, that'll work.

I sent the roughly five-foot-long chain through the loop, creating a pile on the other side, and stopped when the metal hoop on the ground met the shackle around my ankle. Then I stood.

Rolling my shoulders, I loosened my arms and bent to lift the twisted mess of metal. If I heaved it all at the right angle, with enough strength, that ring secured into the cement ground would aid me in snapping the steel circle right off my ankle cuff.

Just a regular deadlift.

Nothing exciting.

Right.

I exhaled slowly, focusing on the task, the metal heavy against my forearms. My thighs began to protest from my squatting position, encouraging me to move. I powered upward, the rusted chains digging into my skin.

And snapping right where I desired at the bottom.

Thank fuck.

My arms protested as I slowly and carefully returned the chains to the ground. The rusty loops had painted my skin an orangish shade that I didn't care for.

Seriously, who owned a dungeon with such archaic bullshit? Arthur would be positively appalled with these accommodations. His underground lair put this place to shame.

Shaking my head, I went to examine the door, again dismayed at the antiquated manufacturing. They'd locked me in here with an old-fashioned latch and padlock. It was as if they wanted me to escape.

Glancing around, I found what I needed in the gross, decrepit bed. The old frame made it easy to twist off one of the legs, providing me with a lead pipe. I weighed it in my hands, testing—

A bloodcurdling scream had my head whipping to the left. *That* was definitely Amara. And I would be killing whoever forced her to make that fucking sound.

This pipe would have to do.

I slid it through the bars of the door—an outdated style they probably kept down here to enable the sick fucks to spy on whatever women they usually kept in the room. Creepy as hell.

A sharp curse from Amara whistled through the air, fueling my adrenaline as I threaded the makeshift crowbar through the metal prongs of the padlock. Anchoring it the way I needed, I used it as a lever to pop the steel apart, the lock falling with a loud clatter against the concrete floor.

Time to move. Because if I could hear Amara, then the bastards hurting her could hear me.

I set the bar down, preferring my hands as weapons, then stepped into the murky area beyond my cell, closing the door behind me. The space reminded me of an old wine cellar with its yellowish lighting and shadowy walls, but the row of cells certainly depicted a far more gruesome picture.

How many girls are down here?

A thought for another time because someone was approaching.

I stepped into an alcove adjacent to my cell, using the gloominess to my advantage.

"I think he's awake," a taunting voice called, footsteps sounding over the slick concrete floor. "Make her scream louder; I want to watch the jackass struggle."

My lips curled. *Oh, there will be a struggle all right.*

The dipshit approaching was so focused on my cell door that he didn't notice me until it was too late. I covered his mouth with one hand, grabbed his hair with the other, and yanked—hard—in opposite directions, snapping his neck.

I had no idea who he was, nor did I care. I let him fall to the floor and followed the sounds of Amara's growls to the open torture area at the end of the corridor.

The scene before me painted my vision in red.

Amara was strapped facedown to a table, her creamy

skin marred with red welts and blood. Everything else I had to ignore, too furious to focus. A man I didn't recognize stood near her mouth and Malcom was between her spread legs.

I didn't think.

I reacted.

I took the flogger from Malcom's hand and slapped his bare chest with it harshly before shoving the handle into his mouth and punching him. He stumbled backward, stunned.

His buddy was faster. He'd pulled up his pants, a gun appearing in his hand, but I caught the jackass before he could lift it. Taking the pistol from him, I unleashed two bullets into his exposed torso in quick succession before turning to fire a shot into Malcom's abdomen. The flogger fell from his mouth as I sent a second bullet into his—thankfully, still-clothed—groin.

Both men went down in a flash, their expressions ones of confused shock.

I tossed the gun onto the table beside all their instruments, most of which were coated in blood—Amara's blood.

Fuck…

If I found her broken, I'd torture these bastards until they begged me to end it. I'd shred them. Shove things inside them the coroner wouldn't be able to remove. Rip them apart with my fucking hands.

Steeling myself for the worst, I focused on her.

And my heart stopped.

She lifted her head to the side and stared up at me with a fierceness that stole my breath, her fury at what they'd been doing a palpable presence.

They'd not shattered her resolve.

No. They'd *enhanced* it.

I unlatched her ankles first, then her waist, followed by her wrists. Her back was bleeding and sticky with unmentionable fluids, her hair matted, her body bruised, but her eyes held the windows to her soul as she rolled off the table onto unsteady feet.

I caught her hips, steadying her as she regained her balance, a curse falling from her bruised lips. "What do you need?" I asked her, knowing this was her time for revenge. Her moment to take out all that pain on two of the assholes who had caused it, and revel in their cries.

"A knife," she rasped, her throat likely raw from screaming.

I hated that I'd not been here sooner, that I'd allowed them so much time alone with her. But wallowing in the past muddied the future, and I refused to do that. Not when I had my warrior before me, asking for my weapon of choice.

There were several scalpels on the table, and three of my daggers. They must have taken those from my clothes with the anticipation of using them.

Well, they were about to be used all right.

I handed one to Amara, leaving the other two within reach on the table should she need another.

She didn't smile. Didn't thank me. But turned to look at the monsters groaning on the floor. While she debated her next move, I assessed the room for security cameras and found none.

This dungeon sucked.

Not that I should complain, as it made it that much easier for us to escape.

But for fuck's sake, the Roses operated a multimillion-dollar slavery scheme, and they knew nothing about proper underground protocols. Or perhaps it was a result of their usual prisoners being scared little girls.

I couldn't wait to watch Amara kill them. They deserved pain. A lot of it.

She started with the jackass who had his dick near her mouth, bending down to draw my knife directly across his throat without a word. Then watched as he choked on his own blood, a look of awe on her face.

Not exactly triumph or satisfaction, but more like wonder at watching life slip away from the monster at her feet. Malcom had curled into the fetal position, mourning the damage to his dick. He seemed completely unaware of his dying friend.

"Who was he?" I wondered out loud.

Amara shook her head, her attention having shifted to the dying senator. She just stared at him, her fingers clutching the blade handle so hard that her knuckles were white.

Malcom remained oblivious, too concerned about his own wounds to see her coming.

A mistake on his part. Because she resembled a naked vigilante goddess, her eyes bright with vengeance, her limbs shaking from the rage building inside her.

"You. Do. Not. Own. Me." She bent to grab a fistful of his hair, forcing him to look at her. "I am not a toy. I am not a fuck doll. I am not a slut. *You* are a monster."

He snorted, then winced and moaned at the injuries he'd sustained. Fucking pansy. This was the part when they all begged for their lives. Irony at its finest because he undoubtedly enjoyed putting others in this position.

How many times had he forced Amara to plead? What about the other women he'd likely violated?

I folded my arms, pleased to see him filling the shoes of his victims. His death should be prolonged and painful, but the choice belonged to my warrior. If she longed for it to be quick, I would respect it. If she wanted to make him scream, I'd happily listen. And if anyone tried to disturb this moment, I'd kill them.

She tugged on his scalp, bending to place her face close to his. "I have something for you to swallow, *Malcom*. I think you'll enjoy it because you're a dirty, filthy bastard."

The words must have been ones he said to her in the past, or maybe even tonight, because the venom pouring from her voice was underlined in experience.

Amara pressed the blade to his lips. "Open wide for me, *slut*." She rammed the knife into his mouth with considerable strength, forcing every inch down his throat. His screams were lost to a horrible gurgling, one that satisfied my need for blood and left Amara watching him without emotion.

His hands lifted, his fingers trying to claw at the item stuck in his mouth, but he couldn't gain purchase on the handle. She'd shoved it in too deep, lodging it inside him with no escape.

"Suck it," she encouraged him. "Enjoy it. Swallow it."

Harsh, dark words that finally brought a hint of feeling to her features. Tears. The wobbling of her lips. A deep, sad exhale.

I pulled her into my arms before the first sob broke, holding her against me and ignoring her soiled state. She needed my strength, my adoration, my *love*.

We weren't done yet, had several others to kill, but she required the pause to regain her focus. I'd do whatever she needed, give her whatever she asked for, and never let her go.

Malcom convulsed, dying out of the corner of my eye. *Good riddance, asshole.*

My arms tightened around Amara, devastated for her and proud at the same time. This was one nightmare of many that she needed to extinguish to reconcile her past and move into the future.

She'd never forget. That was not what this was about. Experiences shaped us, taught us how to live, and influenced who we became.

"He's dead," she whispered.

"He is."

She swallowed, her nails digging into my lower back as she hugged me fiercely. "I killed him."

"You did." I combed my fingers through her tangled strands, wishing I could offer her more. Like clothes. "I'm proud of you, kitten."

"For killing him?"

"No." I pulled away to cup her cheek, wanting to see her eyes. They were still brown from the contacts but glimmering with power. "I'm proud of you for standing up to him, for allowing your strength to lead your actions. You're gorgeous and fierce and the most courageous woman I've ever met. You're amazing,

Amara." *And I think I've fallen in love with you.*

"Gorgeous?" she repeated, glancing down at her current state. "Not at the moment."

"Sometimes beauty isn't about appearance, but what lives inside a person." I pressed my lips to her swollen mouth, then rested my forehead against hers. "We're not done here."

"I know," she whispered. "I want her dead, Killian."

"Good." I slid my palm to her nape, holding her to me for a moment longer. There had to be clothes down here somewhere. We'd find them in—

An explosion rocked the foundation above, followed by two more in quick succession. My lips curled, the sound one of my favorites. "Nikolai is here." He must have been nearby, which could only mean one thing.

Arthur had tasked him as a backup resource for tonight's auction. Knowing Nikolai, when the order went out, he'd picked it up first so he could jump in only as needed. He could have given me a heads-up, but something told me Arthur wanted him to keep me in the dark and act like some sort of babysitter.

A punishment for not acting on his information as

swiftly as he preferred. *Dick.*

Well, at least it worked in my favor.

Another boom sounded upstairs, the walls around us shaking from the impact. "We need to get out of here before something collapses on our heads," I said, noting the escape routes and grabbing my knives. I took her palm with my free hand and pulled her back down the corridor, as this seemed to be a dead end.

But Amara squeezed my hand, tugging me into a narrow pathway that led away from the cells. Trusting her to know her way around, I followed. Sure enough, a set of back stairs appeared. She guided us upward to a panel that controlled a door, and surprised me by entering the code.

"How did you know that?" I asked as we stepped through the threshold into what appeared to be a back room of sorts.

"I watched as Malcom entered it on our way down."

My lips curled. "Clever."

"He always underestimated my intelligence," she said, guiding me through the room and into a concrete hallway. These must have been old servant quarters of some kind because they led to yet another set of stairs.

She crept upward as another grenade went off in the distance, then opened the final door to reveal a more ornate seating area. It was vacant, but her dress lay in tatters on the floor. This must have been where they started their assault.

"Who were the other guys?" I wondered out loud again.

"They were friends Malcom knew from the party. Taviv gave the one a gun after he volunteered to help teach me a lesson, which was a little weird. But yeah, I've seen them before. However, never, uh, like that." She opened a closet filled with jackets and pulled a peacoat off a hanger. It hit her midthigh, so it worked almost as a dress.

I didn't bother trying anything on. I'd just have to face these assholes in my boxers.

"Where to?" I asked her. "Where would they hide?" Because they had to be panicking as a result of Nikolai's explosions.

"The office." She was already moving, her spine straight and her strides determined. I twirled my blades in my palms as I followed, ready to cut anyone who stepped in our path.

The grenades had stopped going off, either because Nikolai was already inside or because he'd run out of firepower. Likely the former.

Amara paused in the hallway, just outside a double door, her shoulders tensed.

This must be the office.

With a nod, as if reassuring herself, she shoved the doors open and froze on the threshold. A gasp fluttered from her mouth as my own jaw hit the floor.

I'd anticipated the potential for an ambush.

But not this macabre scene.

Clarissa and Geoff Rose were already dead, their throats slit from ear to ear. And between them sat a legal-sized envelope with Amara's name scrawled across it.

And below it read, *I'm proud of you, Daughter. See you soon. Assad.*

AMARA

Dearest Amara,

If you're reading this, which I suspect you are, then you've passed the final stage in your training. I couldn't be prouder of the woman you've become. It's a triumphant feeling to watch your progeny grow and defeat those standing in her way, to reach the top of an empire.

Creating you is one of my biggest victories. You're perfect in every way—conniving, strong, and willing to do whatever it takes to win. My daughter to the end. I only wish your mother could see you now. I told her your future, how I intended to mold you into a woman of power and status. And here you are, doing exactly as I planned.

Enclosed you will find everything you need to

succeed in your new position, all the documents of your past and future, and the details you'll require to run the former Rose family business. I've taken the liberty of cleaning up the utter mess Clarissa has left behind. All her previous employees are retiring as I write this, leaving you with a fresh start—my gift to you.

My primary goal was to provide the building blocks you needed to reign, and here you are, my darling Amara, standing at the top of one of the world's oldest organizations. With all the assets of a famous former senator as well.

I doubt many other parents have ever gifted their child with such success, but I've always felt you deserved the best.

I'll be in touch soon, once you're settled in. Should you need me in the interim, reach me through Taviv— he is your older brother, after all.

Your father,
Amir

P.S. Welcome to the family, Bedivere. I wasn't sure

about you at first, but you've proven to be an admirable
companion for my Amara. Treat her right.

I read the letter three times before I finally set it
down to stare at Killian. "What. The. Fuck?"

He had spread the other contents of the envelope
out over the desk, ignoring the corpses of Clarissa
and Geoff behind him. They were situated in the
wingback chairs, portraying a brutal throne scene with
their ruined clothes and dead eyes.

But I honestly couldn't even focus on them with
the bombshell Amir had dropped in my lap. "He's my
father?"

"It would appear so, yes." Killian slid over a birth
certificate with my name on it, listing Amir Assad as
the father and Flora Assad as the mother. "Then there's
this." He handed me a financial document showing an
initial transfer of funds from Amir to Clarissa, the
transaction details stating it was a payment for my
care.

More transactions followed in a monthly pattern,
the sums widening my eyes.

"And these," Killian said, his tone holding a

darkness that had me uncertain as to whether or not I wanted to see the papers in his hand. But he gave them to me anyway.

Brief instructions. All in writing. All depicting exactly what Amir wanted done to me in terms of my *training*. He even provided a timeline and a list of desired candidates, all of whom he instructed Clarissa to invite to my sixteenth birthday. The night that changed everything.

My stomach churned with the details.

I felt dizzy.

Overwhelmed.

Shocked.

Abused.

I sat in the chair behind the desk, clutching the letter as if it held all the answers. And yet it told me nothing at all. "What empire? What organization? What the fuck is he talking about?"

Killian remained quiet, his attention on more of the documents from the never-ending envelope.

"It seems he's transferred all of Malcom's assets to you. As well as the Rose estate and all their former funds, of which there is a great deal." His lips flattened, his dark eyes lifting to mine. "If I'm understanding all of this, it means he's chosen you to lead the Rose family legacy. To run the trafficking rings and the several other illegal affairs they've managed throughout the last few centuries."

"That's not going to happen."

"It seems that it's already happening. You own everything, Amara." He set the envelope down, his expression shuttered. "This is all yours."

"I don't want it."

"I don't think Assad cares." He gestured to the documents. "It's already done."

"Then we need to undo it." Because I didn't want any of this. I only desired freedom, not to be the queen of an illegal empire. "I'm not Clarissa."

"I know."

"I'm not accepting this." I pushed off the chair, swaying from the onslaught of sensation. Fuck, I was going to be sick. And I smelled. And I ached. And, oh God, I just wanted a shower and to lie down, and to forget everything.

Forget the way Malcom had touched me.

The feel of his flogger against my back.

The burning that followed when his fucked-up friend poured his glass of scotch over my wounds.

The agony of Malcom roughly toweling off my back afterward to wipe up most of the mess.

The way he *tasted* afterward when he tried to kiss me.

I shuddered, needing it all to end. To not believe a word of this. To disappear. "I don't want this," I said, likely repeating myself. "Killian, I don't accept it."

"We'll figure it out."

"There's nothing to figure out!" I shouted. "I'm not accepting it!"

"Amara—"

"No!" I dug my palms into my eyes, striving for control, trying to remember how to breathe. I'd killed Malcom. But Amir—*my father*—was still very much alive. And apparently, he expected me to take over the Rose family legacy.

I shook my head, my abdomen clenching tightly.

A low whistle sounded, causing me to freeze. "Do I even want to know?" a male voice drawled.

Frowning, I lowered my hands to find a tall, dark-haired man leaning against the door frame in a black leather jacket. His chiseled features reminded me a bit of Killian, in that both men had an edge to them, in a classically handsome sort of way.

"Nik, way to arrive late to the party," Killian replied, turning to face him.

"Yeah?" He hooked his thumb over his shoulder. "The living area back there is littered with bodies. Pretty sure I crashed the party, man."

"How many?"

He shrugged. "Thirty. Forty. Grenades are messy things. Although, a few tried to make a break for it outside. Gave me a chance to play a little target practice."

"What about the girls?" I asked, my heart in my throat. *They didn't deserve this. None of them did.*

"I found several of them in another room lined up like cattle. Killed their handlers, but left the girls alive."

I swallowed. "How many g-girls?"

"Uh, nine or ten, why?"

Relief washed over me. Clarissa must have moved them to the auction area, readying them for the bids.

"She's worried you killed some innocents," Killian replied when I didn't.

The other man snorted. "What do you think I am? An amateur? I checked the room before I tossed the grenade in there. It was filled with assholes in masks with placards." He looked at Killian. "Dude, where the fuck are your clothes?"

"I thought you didn't want to know?" Killian countered, his brow arching.

"The curiosity is killing me." His lips twitched. "And you look like hell run over. Nice ornament, by the way." He nodded at the metal cuff around Killian's ankle. "What happened? You get distracted? Caught with your pants down—literally?"

"More like ambushed in a stairwell," he replied dryly.

His friend nodded slowly, his amusement palpable. "Good thing I came to your rescue."

"Yes, clearly I needed it. Oh wait, your little explosion show almost took down the house while we were in the basement dungeon."

"Dungeon?" he repeated, his interest flaring. "Show me."

"It's a shit show; you wouldn't be amused. Their supplies date back to, like, the nineteenth century.

Which helped us out, but it's a total clusterfuck down there." Killian sounded so appalled, while all I could think about was what happened down there.

Malcom's flogger hitting my flesh.

His demands that I obey.

His friends laughing.

I shuddered, the too-fresh memory overtaking my mind and melting into what I'd done to them. How good it felt to slide the blade across that asshole's throat. I'd channeled Killian with that move, having seen him do it at the masquerade ball. But Malcom's death had been all me. He wanted me to suck things? Well, I returned the favor in kind.

He's dead.

The reminder empowered me until I glanced at the papers on the desk.

This had all been a setup, Amir's fucked-up way of training me for a position in management. What did he expect me to do? Slide right in and play the part of the new Madam? No. Hell no. I refused. I wanted to free all the women from their lives of agony and burn this fucking place to the ground.

And I can, I realized. *Because it's mine.*

"We're going to destroy it," I whispered, my gaze landing on Killian. "I want to burn this fucking house to the ground." He'd been in the middle of saying something to his friend, but I didn't care. "Get all the girls outside. Then we're burning this place down," I told them both.

"Bonfire," his buddy replied, sounding intrigued. "It'll please the cleanup crew."

"Are you sure, Amara?" Killian asked, his brow creasing.

"Do you think I want to keep this place?" Because if he did, then he clearly didn't know me as well as I thought.

"No. But you could reorganize it, turn it into a place of good."

"There is no good here. It's pure evil. And I want to demolish it." Every damn inch needed to be cleansed, and this was the only way. "It'll send a clear message to Amir that I'm not interested in playing a role in his fucked-up game. I want out."

He studied me for a long moment, then nodded. "If that's what you want, that's what we'll do." He stepped closer, his palm catching the back of my neck to hold me before him. "But I have two conditions." When I opened my mouth to argue, he pressed his thumb to my lips. "First, all those documents come with us. You may want to destroy them and run from this, but there's a history there that might one day save your life. We need them."

"And your second?" I mumbled against his thumb.

"It's going to take over an hour to clear the house, so while Nikolai works on that, you and I will find a shower and some clothes to change into."

"When did I volunteer for that?" Nikolai asked from behind Killian.

"You volunteered the second you took Arthur's assignment." He glanced over his shoulder. "Besides, we both know you have a soft spot for trafficking victims, Nik."

His friend merely shrugged. "I'll call Ava for some recommendations. Meet me out front in sixty and we'll light her up." He disappeared, leaving me alone with Killian.

And the dead bodies.

And the papers.

Killian's dark eyes returned to mine, his gaze

searching. "We're going to find him, kitten."

"Amir?"

He nodded. "He may be your father, but what he did to you can't go unpunished." His brows crinkled, his pupils studying mine intently. "You know that, right?"

"Amir destroyed my life. Set me up to run a criminal organization I never wanted. Had me raped. Abused. *Pissed* on. And so many other wretched things. I want him dead, Killian. Fuck whatever all this is; I want him to pay for it. In blood."

His grip on my neck tightened, his opposite hand going to my hip to pull me closer. "There's my Amara." His mouth brushed mine. "My warrior." Another kiss, this one deeper, hotter. I was bleeding, fresh off killing two men, and just found out Amir Assad was my father, and Killian still wanted me. Still adored me. Still cared.

That undid something inside me, some sort of final barrier I'd kept locked up around my heart. And a flood of sensation came over me. All of it for the man who held me in his arms, protecting me, adoring me, respecting me.

He literally saved my life.

Yes, I had escaped my hell, but he taught me that I didn't need to run. He encouraged me to be free, to fight, to face my nightmares head-on and destroy them. Killian was my everything, the one who completed me, the one who pushed me to fly.

With him, I could do anything.

"I love you," I whispered, the words falling from me on a cascade of emotion. I grabbed his bare shoulders, needing to hold on, afraid and thrilled and overwhelmed. "I love you, Killian."

He pressed his forehead to mine, his breath hot against my lips. "I love you, too, Amara." Softly spoken, but heartfelt and true and so incredibly warm.

He walked me backward until my ass hit the desk, then lifted me on top of it.

"I shouldn't do this, not after what they did, but I want you, Amara." He unbuttoned the jacket, letting it fall open to reveal my breasts, his gaze roaming over me as if to assure himself I was okay. "It's so damn wrong, but..."

"It's what I need," I whispered, finishing the sentence for him. "They barely touched me, Killian, but it was enough that I need you to erase the memory." I finished removing the soiled coat and threw it across the room, the assaulting scents from the dungeon below seeming to disappear with it.

All of Malcom's attentions had been to my back, leaving my front unmarred. He'd really only just begun when Killian showed up, the men having been waiting for an audience to hear them before truly hurting me. The flogging had been the worst, enough to leave me chilled. And now I craved Killian's heat.

"Fuck me," I told him. "Bring me back to you. To us. To who we are meant to be together." I wanted him to ruin me for anyone else, including those of my past. He may have called it wrong, but I considered it to be right. "Make me yours, Killian."

"You are mine, kitten," he whispered, stepping in between my spread thighs. "Just as I'm yours."

"Show me." I leaned back on the desk, balancing on my palms, the papers scattered beneath me. But they no longer mattered. There were two dead bodies in the room, a sea of pain, and nightmares painting the walls. And still, I didn't care.

Killian's boxers slid down his thighs, revealing

his gorgeous cock, perfectly erect and ready for me. I yearned for the darkness that lived within him, the part of him that thrived on violence and enjoyed spilling blood. I needed that man, my dark knight, the one who could erase everything around me and take me to a plane of nonexistence.

"Hard," I told him. "Rough. I need you to hurt me, Killian." To help me erase the memory of Malcom and replace this night with memories of Killian alone.

"Only in the best ways," he promised, thrusting into me and filling me in the most delicious manner. "I'll erase them all, Amara. Everyone who ever touched you. You'll never think of them again."

"Yes," I moaned, arching into him, accepting him into every part of me. Not just physically, but spiritually. I allowed him to love me, to worship me, to understand me, to complete me.

I balanced against the desk with one hand, my other going to his nape, my nails digging in as he took my mouth with a ferocity I felt to my very soul. *Mine.*

He set a punishing pace, exactly as I requested, his hips driving into mine with a force that hurt. The wood beneath me creaked, his grip on my waist harsh as he moved me the way he desired, taking and giving what we both needed.

"Killian," I breathed against his lips, so close to release, my body on fire for him.

"Are you going to come for me, Amara?" He licked the inside of my mouth, one of his hands sliding to my mound to thumb my throbbing clit. "Are you going to milk me with that sweet, tight pussy, kitten?" He pinched my nub, sending a spike of pain and pleasure through me, leaving me quivering against him. "Say my name again."

"Killian," I moaned, convulsing. "My Killian."

"And who am I?" he pressed, his mouth hot against mine.

"My knight." I bowed off the desk, only to be slammed back down by his hips, the move agonizingly perfect. "My Sir Bedivere."

"And you're my warrior," he whispered. "My beautiful, fierce Amara."

I came apart at his words, all the torment from before releasing on a wave of relief that only Killian could evoke. It hurt. It soothed. It tore me apart. It put me back together. And feeling him erupt inside me only intensified the moment, making it all the more perfect and right, with a heavy dose of scandalousness that sent me crashing into euphoric bliss.

Everything left me on a contented sigh. All the torture. Malcom's harsh treatment. Today's murders. Amir's games. The documents. None of it mattered. Only Killian and his heavy groans against my neck, the feel of his hands roaming over me, of his seed spilling inside me.

Utopia.

My future had finally arrived, and I wanted every minute of it with this man by my side.

And the way he whispered my name now told me he felt the same.

He found me. Held me captive. But I captured the most valuable item of all—the heart of an assassin. Of *my* assassin. And I would never be letting him go.

"I love you," I said again, solidifying our unspoken promise to one another.

"I love you, too," he replied, his mouth taking mine.

Maybe Amir was right. Maybe I did belong at the top. But it would be his throne I went for next.

With an armed knight at my side.

EPILOGUE

AMARA

The Greek cafe reminded me a bit of the restaurant Killian and I once dined at in Cairo. It was the little touches, like the way the waiter excitedly spoke English and the very helpful host who called me *Mrs. Dagger*.

But the company this time was a lot less charming.

I swirled my wine, waiting.

Amir would arrive any minute now.

It'd taken us ten months to track him down, and two more to plan this moment. Killian waited outside, his voice warm in my ear as he murmured, "I do love that dress on you, kitten."

My lips curled at his words. "I know."

He was watching me from a sniper rifle one roof over, just in case things went south. But I knew

they wouldn't. I'd arranged everything, including the meeting.

"Daddy dearest just appeared," Killian informed me softly. "He's alone. No Taviv."

I expected as much.

From what I'd gathered over the last year, Taviv wasn't nearly as compliant as he'd first appeared. I still didn't fully understand him, but with a father like ours, I suspected his position in this life wasn't one of his choosing. That didn't mean I would allow him to live indefinitely, but he could live for now, while I kept a close watch on him.

Amir, however, would die.

Today.

"You ready, kitten?" Killian asked, his low voice seductive.

We both enjoyed this lethal game. It had turned into our version of foreplay over the last year as we hunted down everyone involved in the trafficking syndicate. One of the many items Amir had gifted me was Clarissa's client list. Killian had promptly turned it into a kill list. And I'd helped him cross off each mark.

"I am," I said as Amir walked through the front door. He greeted the host, then followed him to a table in the corner, the one he always chose, which meant his wine was already waiting for him. I finished my own glass, watching him and grinning as he took a sip. "Time to play, sir. Wish me luck."

"You don't need it," Killian replied, his tone amused.

I picked up my purse, smiling. "True." Because Amir was exactly where I wanted him. He used to terrify me, make my blood run cold with fear, but I'd spent the last year learning everything I could about him. And today I would be using it all to my advantage.

He glanced up as I approached, his arched brow the only indication of his surprise as I slid into the chair across from him. And set my purse on the table. "Father," I greeted him, sarcasm heavy in my voice.

"Hello, Amara," he replied, tilting his head to the side. "You look… colorful."

I glanced at the tattoos running up my right arm and smiled. "Do you like them?" Killian did. I added a new one after every kill, picking an item from each memory to print on my arm. Nothing obvious, just little things. Like the wine glass sitting in front of Amir. That'd be my next object.

"Not my first choice, but you've proven to be quite rebellious, so they're fitting." He toasted me and took another sip.

"You don't approve of the Scarlet Foundation?" I asked innocently. It was the organization I'd created with the Rose family fortune. "We've helped over a thousand trafficking victims this year. I thought you'd be proud. I mean, you did put me in charge, after all."

He smirked. "Actually, I am proud. I told you it was yours to do with as you pleased, and you have. It's not what your legacy preferred, but that's the beauty of painting your own canvas."

The waiter arrived with Amir's meal, having been prepared in expectation of his arrival. "Would you like anything, Mrs. Dagger?"

"No, thank you," I replied, smiling. "I have everything I need."

Amir dismissed him with a wave and began cutting up his fish. "Your mother would be quite pleased, you know."

"Would she?"

"Oh, yes." He took a bite, his eyes closing on a sigh of contentment. "Mmm…" He chewed and swallowed, following it with some more wine. "She always tried to best me, your mother. Failed at every turn because I wasn't ready then. But I think I might be now."

"Are you saying she tried to kill you?" I asked, trying to translate his cryptic statements.

He shrugged. "On occasion. It was more that she tried to trick me; it's why you moved so much as a child. She was hiding you from me." He chuckled as if amused. "One of the best games of cat and mouse of my lifetime. And I won, of course. She was so mad when I sent you away, but it was for the best. You wouldn't be who you are today had I not taken those measures."

"And who exactly do you think I am today?" I wondered.

"A chameleon," he replied. "You can play the role of a lady, a deviant, a warrior, or even a black widow, all within the span of minutes without breaking stride. You're walking perfection, Amara. My finest achievement. Which means I can die knowing you're carrying on the family name the way it deserves to be." He finished his glass, setting it aside and smiling at me. "The pawn has finally become a queen. And she's taken down the king."

I stared at him. "I had no idea you were so fond of riddles."

But I understood what he was saying.

He knew about the poison in his drink, had accepted it with pride.

"Why?" I asked. "Why drink it?"

"Because it's that or take a bullet from your Bedivere, and this seems much more peaceful." He ate another bite of his fish, humming happily in that odd way of his as he swallowed. "It's my time anyway. You and Taviv are both in a position to lead, meaning I've done my job and I can finally accept my fate. My work here is done. And you being here, handing me my death, confirms that."

"You're nothing like I expected," I admitted, confused by his acquiescence. This had to be a trick of some kind, a ploy to lull me into a false sense of comfort.

"The smartest play is always the one others will

least expect, Amara." He picked up his water, taking a long gulp and setting it down, relaxing into his chair on an exhale. It was the only sign that the potassium cyanide was working. It usually took a few minutes to start feeling the shortness of breath, and it appeared to finally be setting in.

He took another short breath and winced. "Will you stay with me? Until the end?"

"Do you want that?" I asked, oddly less enthused about this plan than I had been moments ago.

"I would... like that." He gave me a weak smile, clasping his hands in his lap. "Tell me... your... next move."

"Today? Or in general?"

"General," he replied, his voice raspier than before.

"I... I'm working with Congressman Winters on an anti-trafficking initiative." I didn't know why I told him that, but I was proud of the alliance. He was the congressman from the masquerade ball. I learned from looking through Clarissa's notes that she listed him as a threat because of his policy stances, which made him my immediate ally. "I'm also hoping to expand the Scarlet Foundation internationally."

He nodded. "G-good." He seemed pleased, which was fucking weird. "Wh-what else? B-Bedivere?" He convulsed violently, his eyes closing for a moment and then lifting to reveal dilated pupils.

"We have an understanding," I said. "He does his job, I do mine, and sometimes we work together." Specifically when it involved a client from Clarissa's list.

"Y-you're h-happy?" he stuttered, his throat working hard over the words.

The question gave me pause. Because yes, I was, happier than I'd ever been. And not because of this asshole, but because of Killian.

Except I never would have met Killian had Amir not played me as a puppet in his grand play. So in some sick and twisted way, I owed him for introducing us.

"E-everything... happens... for... a reason," he managed on an exhale, his lips turning blue from the oxygen deprivation. "I... you... success."

"I am who I am because of my own decisions, not because of what you've done to me," I said, tired of him claiming my life as if he'd orchestrated every piece of it. And maybe he had, but fuck, I survived because of *me*, not him. I thrived because of Killian. Amir merely put pieces in place, pieces that *hurt*, and watched me overcome them. That made him a monster, not a master creator.

His lips curled. "Per... fection." His eyes closed, his breath shuddering out of him. I waited for another inhale, but none came. The look of serenity on his face unsettled me, yet pleased me at the same time.

He'd accepted his fate.

And... died.

Without tricks, without protests, just a semi-normal conversation underlined in pride.

"Amara?" Killian murmured, his voice a shock to my heart that I didn't know I needed. It sent a wave of warmth through my chilly veins, awakening me from my stupor.

"He's dead," I replied. Or almost, anyway. It'd take a few more minutes for the cardiac arrest to complete, but even if he sought medical help now, he'd never be the same. And it was doubtful they could revive him.

I studied his face once more, noting the subtle similarities to my own that I missed before—the shape of his jaw, his nose, the color of his skin. I bore all those traits, and likely more.

My will to survive.

My intelligence.

My desire to defy expectations.

Amir possessed all of those in spades and, apparently, passed them on to me. But I owned my future, not him.

And now he could never touch me again.

I pushed away from the table, purse in hand, and headed outside.

"It's done," I said softly, more to myself than to Killian. A weight lifted from my shoulders, from my heart. I could finally move on. Live. Enjoy. Just *be*.

"Where to next, kitten?" Killian asked as he joined me outside, his dark hair artfully windswept from being up on the other roof. He must have left his sniper rifle somewhere in the building, because his hands were empty.

"Wherever you want to go," I replied, smiling.

"Cairo?" he suggested, eyebrows waggling. "I seem to recall you wanting to see the pyramids."

I still did. Very much. "We'll need new identities,"

I warned.

"Not an issue. How do you feel about Scarlet Mark?"

I frowned. "Scarlet Mark?" That didn't match any of his previous aliases.

He wrapped his arm around me, pulling me alongside him down the empty cobblestone street. "It's a play on your first alias of Scarlet Rosalind. You were quite literally my Scarlet Mark."

"And what would you go by?" I wondered, leaning into him.

"Dagger Mark, of course."

"You really think people will believe that name?"

"Oh, kitten, haven't you realized?" He glanced at me sideways. "Money buys you anything you want. Including sexy little dances from redheads with tattoos in a nightclub."

My skin heated at the reminder of our first night together. The danger and intrigue, the pure sex radiating between us. "Are you requesting a follow-up?" I asked, my voice dropping to a sultry purr I knew he liked.

"Without the ketamine this time, yes."

"Okay, Sir Bedivere," I replied, smiling up at him. "I think Scarlet Mark would be happy to oblige."

"Yeah?" He pulled me into an alleyway between two buildings and pushed me up against a wall. "What else will Scarlet Mark give me? Because I think she owes me a blow job."

"Does she?" I pressed my palms to his abdomen, drawing my nails down to his belt. "You'll need a knife."

"Mmm, you're right. I will. She might try to bite."

I nodded. "She definitely will."

A dagger appeared against my side, his hands always working magic. "You want to play, kitten?"

"Always."

"Good. Then be a good girl and get on your knees."

My lips curled in anticipation. "Yes, sir."

ABOUT THE AUTHOR

USA Today Bestselling Author Lexi C. Foss loves to play in dark worlds, especially the ones that bite. She lives in Atlanta, Georgia with her husband and their furry children. When not writing, she's busy crossing items off her travel bucket list, or chasing eclipses around the globe. She's quirky, consumes way too much coffee, and loves to swim.

Where To Find Lexi:
www.LexiCFoss.com

Made in the USA
Monee, IL
01 May 2020